Daughters of Avalon

Book Three

The Wizard's Book

Darryl A. Jouett

To Lawrence and Claudette –

Thank you for showing me that no matter how dark it may get, the light always finds a way to make things right again.

I would also like to extend a special 'Thank You' to Doug Eagler and Shawn Sims...just rest assured that your characters in this book are nothing like you – they're much taller!

I wish to thank the people who helped with the editing process for this series of books: Amy Schardein, Sherry Hoffman, and Claudette Jouett. Last, but certainly not least, my wonderful wife Melissa, who offered opinions, advice, and great ideas; but most importantly put up with my endless rants and for that I am eternally grateful!

Also by Darryl A. Jouett

Daughters of Avalon

Daughters of Avalon: The Shadow King

Table of Contents

Prologue

Merlin pulled himself along the ground until he located a dense growth of shrubs. He tried to conceal himself within the tightly woven branches; the thorns and prickly leaves cutting angrily into his flesh. He struggled to steady his breathing as he heard the King's Riders quickly approaching. His lungs were on fire and they cried out for oxygen; indeed, the urge to take in great measures of the cool night air almost overrode his need to maintain silence. His fate would be sealed if he were to be captured now.

He had fallen from his mount more than an hour ago and was now attempting to make his escape on foot. The Riders were excellent trackers, however. While the darkness aided Merlin in his efforts of evading his hunters, their combined skill only granted him a half mile lead on them – until now. He had tripped on an exposed root and tumbled down a ravine, twisting his ankle in the process. Now the Riders were upon him, a mere three feet away from his hiding place.

"He has to be here!" the leader of the group said to the other two. He kept his voice just above a whisper so as to not give away their position. "There is no trace of the wizard beyond this point," he continued. "He might be hiding somewhere nearby."

"Is it not possible that he formed one of his portals?" a second Rider asked as he tried to calm his horse. "I have heard it said that he prefers to travel that way."

"I doubt it," the leader answered. "Think about it – when was the last time that any of us witnessed him using magic? Two, maybe three months ago? No, I believe that the rumors about him losing his powers are true. He is close. I can feel it!"

"Then let us ride on," the third soldier said anxiously. "He cannot have gotten far!"

The leader gave the area one more cursory glance before he signaled for the others to follow him. Merlin listened intently as the sound of their horses' hooves grew faint in the distance. When he was positive that they had gone he pulled himself from his makeshift hideaway. Thorny branches pulled and tugged at his hair and beard, but he did not cry out. He was well aware of how sound traveled at night, and he did not want to alert his pursuers. He stumbled away from the bush and hobbled over to a nearby tree. Leaning against it for support, he finally allowed himself to gulp in great lungfuls of air while he accessed his present situation.

His ankle was throbbing, and he could feel it swelling up inside of his boot. He put some weight upon it, testing it out gingerly, and the jolt of pain that coursed throughout his body from that single act nearly caused him to lose consciousness. Sweat fell from his forehead and caused his eyes to burn as he ran his hand across his face to remove the salty droplets. Merlin began to think about his next course of action and gasped in surprise as the answer appeared right before his very eyes.

Nestled amongst the trees, almost hidden from view, was a small cottage. The shutters were drawn, but he could see a sliver of light through the small slits of the wooden window screens. Its roof was made of thatch and its walls were of stone and wood, but they were now overgrown with a carpet of moss and ivy. The coat of green softened the cottage's hard surfaces, and the large array of flowers that surrounded the enchanting little home seemed to beckon him toward the front door.

Merlin took a tentative step toward the cottage, but he was unable to maintain his balance. Inadvertently, he put too much weight onto his ankle and fell to the ground, crying out loudly as the pain raced from his injured leg straight to his brain.

The front door of the small cottage creaked open and Merlin was abruptly bathed in a bright, warm light. He threw his hands up to his face, peeking through his fingers in an effort to soften the light's blinding glare. A diminutive form appeared in the doorway and stopped short, as the person in shadow took notice of Merlin sprawled out upon the ground. The wizard heard a gasp of shock emanate from the silhouette, and he lowered his hand so the person could see him more clearly.

"Can you...," Merlin groaned, "...can you help me? Please?!"

"Who *are* you?" the voice was that of a young woman.

"I...I took a fall...from my...from my horse," Merlin said, ignoring her question. "I need help...my ankle..."

He could see her staring down at him, and then she carefully surveyed the surrounding woods. He made no sudden movements; instead, he remained perfectly still, in order for her to fully take in what had occurred just outside her doorway. Apparently satisfied that this was not some sort of trick, she walked over to Merlin and knelt down beside him.

"I...I won't hurt you," he said gritting his teeth from the pain. "Truly, I...I mean you no harm."

"I do not believe that you would be much of a threat in your current condition," she said. "And I am more than capable of taking care of myself."

"I'm sure that you are," Merlin said. He tried to smile, but another wave of pain took him and he breathed in sharply from the force of it.

"We need to get you inside," she said concerned. "If I support you, can you make your way into the cottage?"

"I...I think so," Merlin grunted. "Yes, I...I think that I can...can make it."

She took his arm and placed it across her shoulder, and then she took her own arm and wrapped it around his waist. Carefully, she guided the injured mage up onto his feet; helping him take slow, plodding steps out of the chill night air and into the warmth and safety of her home. The cottage was modestly furnished, but there was a charm about the place that put Merlin instantly at ease. His hostess led him to a large, overstuffed chair, and lowered him gently into it. As she fussed about ensuring that he was comfortable, Merlin took the opportunity to take in her features.

She was slightly taller than he was, and of medium build. When she glanced at him he could see that her eyes were a warm shade of blue-green with flecks of gold that seemed to dance in each iris. High-arched eyebrows gave her face an exotic look; which was in stark contrast to her pale skin and honey-brown hair. She wore her hair long and over her shoulders, as was the traditional manner, barely concealing the pointy tips of her elongated ears.

"You're Sidhe," Merlin whispered. She stared at him for a moment, studying him, and then she smiled warmly.

"You are quite observant," she said. "Nothing gets past you, evidently!"

"You would be surprised," Merlin said, chuckling softly.

"Well," his benefactor said as the concern returned to her voice, "that must have been some tumble that you took from your animal. Did he throw you into the brambles?"

"No," Merlin said as he absently pulled a thorny twig from his hair. "I...I did that all by myself."

"I see," she said as she stood back up. "My name is Lissa." She walked over to the door and closed it before turning to face him again. "Can I offer you anything? Food or drink?"

"Some water," Merlin said, "...some water would be nice. Thank you."

"Water it is then," Lissa smiled. She watched him for a moment, the worry more than evident on her face. "I am afraid that I am not skilled in the healing arts, but I know of someone who is. He does not live far from here and I could..."

"No," Merlin said quickly, "that...that won't be necessary! I just need to rest...let my ankle calm down a bit. An hour or two and I will be on my way!"

"If you insist," Lissa said as she made her way to the kitchen. She took a cup down from a cabinet and filled it with some water from a pitcher on the counter. "I happened to notice several Riders wearing the Gorias crest outside my cottage not too long ago," she said as she walked over and handed Merin the cup of water. "It is strange to see them about at such a late hour; do you not agree?"

Merlin took the cup from her and drained it quickly. When she offered up the pitcher again he held out his cup, thanking her as she filled it for a second time.

"So," Lissa pressed, "you have no idea why those Riders are out there – who they might be looking for?"

There was a peculiar taste in the back of Merlin's throat, and he coughed several times in an attempt to clear it before answering. "No," he lied, "none whatsoever."

"Please," Lissa said sternly as she stared down at her guest. "I am taking a great risk in bringing you into my home. Everyone knows that those men are expert trackers. If they are out in these woods, at this time of night, then it is more likely than not that they are searching for someone. So, I ask you again; would that someone happen to be you?"

Merlin eyed Lissa over the brim of his cup as he finished his drink. As he took the cup away from his mouth he noticed that his hands were shaking. *I need to rest,* he thought to himself. He looked back at her and shrugged his shoulders. "They are looking for me," he answered.

"They wore the crest of King Lathos," Lissa said again. "What could you have done to garner not one, but *three* of his pursuers?"

"Let's just say," Merlin whispered as his voice began to grow raspy, "that the king and I do not see eye to eye on a number of topics..." He rubbed his eyes with his free hand as his vision began to grow blurry, and the pain in his ankle now seemed to be spreading throughout his entire body. "I...I'm sorry," he croaked, "but I...I seem to...I can't...!"

Merlin's hand fell away from his face as an intense feeling of dread gripped his heart. His eyes darted around the room hastily before finally settling on Lissa, who was looking at him with a cruel smile upon her lips. He tried to stand, but his arms and legs refused to work. When he attempted to speak, all that issued from his lips was a hissing sound.

"Let me take that from you, Merlin!" The Sidhe said as she walked over to his chair and took the cup from his hand. His fingers remained curled up as though he still had possession of it, and his eyes moved back and forth as a single thought rang out over and over in his head.

How did she know my name? he wondered fearfully.

"You would be amazed at the large number of toxic plants and herbs there are in this small valley," Lissa said matter-of-factly as she walked over to the counter and washed out Merlin's cup. "Take the assortment that I placed in your drink, for example. They are quite nasty; quite nasty indeed!" She turned and faced the wizard, and he could see that her face looked a little different – her eyes had changed color and her ears were no longer sticking out from her hair.

"First," she said gleefully, "there is a paralyzing effect that overwhelms the entire body. It is what you are experiencing right now. Unable to move, unable to speak – you are a prisoner within your own body!"

As she came back over and knelt beside his chair, he could see that her hair was a rich chestnut brown. "I would not worry myself about that if I were you," she said malevolently, "that only lasts for a few hours. It is what will happen next that should concern you.

"Once the paralysis wears off, your body will go into a state of hypersensitivity, as though every nerve ending is on fire! For the next three days, you will be in such extreme pain that you will beg for death. Finally, when your mind is at its breaking point, the elixir that I fed you will be at its most lethal – your heart will literally explode within your chest!"

There was a knock at the door and she got up and went over to it, opening it and allowing King Lathos' men entry. She closed the door behind them and turned to face Merlin once again, her transformation now fully complete.

Morgan le Fay walked over to a corner of the room and kicked away a carpet from the floor. Underneath the rug was a stone slab that was inset within the boards. She instructed the three men to remove the heavy piece of masonry, and when they did, a tomb of stone was revealed beneath it.

"Take the old man and place him inside the sarcophagus," Morgan said icily, "face down!"

As the Riders did as they were told, Morgan laid down beside the opening and stared down at the back of Merlin's head. "I want you to know, old friend, that what I am doing to *you* is far more merciful than what I have planned for your precious little Elementals," she said smiling viciously. "Before the pain takes you and destroys your mind, I want you to envision the worst possible torment that I can unleash upon them – and then multiply it by a thousand! You never should have crossed me, and they should never have gotten in my way. Now they are going to suffer."

Morgan stood up and brushed the wrinkles from her gown. She glared down at Merlin, laying within the tomb, one last time before she turned toward the three men who stood silently by awaiting her instructions.

"Seal it," she said coldly.

1. Monsters among Us

Although he weighed nearly six hundred pounds, Erik moved silently through the forest; weaving in and out among the trees, his wings pulled in tightly against his back. He made his way toward a clearing and stopped at the edge of the tree line. He surveyed the area intensely; his keen eyesight on full alert for the slightest bit of movement. Detecting nothing unusual, he inhaled deeply in an attempt to pick up his quarry's scent, but he was unsuccessful in this effort, as well. Even with the wind blowing into his face all he could detect was the stench of singed flesh – a result of being battered by lightning when he launched his initial attack upon Annalise and the others.

He had already taken down three of them – Zoe and Eryn fell first. Their crude efforts at trying to incapacitate him with a giant water spout had failed miserably. Taking them out of the fight had been child's play. Annalise, however, proved to be more of a challenge. He had pursued her on foot and in the air for more than an hour before they eventually faced off against one another. The Aether had met hs brute force head on with the sheer power of nature itself – literally striking him down several times with bolts of lightning. Magic was the only resort left to him and having used it, Erik was finally able to bring her to her knees and put an end to the conflict. Now, only Blair and Angelica remained.

He stood up on his hind legs, extending his nose up into the sky, dragging in the air once more with the hope of picking up a tell-tale whiff of one of the two girls. His senses ineffective, he decided to throw caution to the wind and enter the clearing. Hesitation, he knew, emboldened the enemy. Remaining upright, he made his way toward the middle of the open expanse. Erik took a look around; and satisfied that all was well, he continued on across the field. He had taken just a few tentative steps forward when he felt the dirt shifting under his feet. It was at that moment that he realized that he had walked right into a trap.

He could feel himself being pulled under, the earth literally devouring him, and he struggled angrily in an attempt to free himself. He dug his claws into the ground seeking purchase, but it was as though he were trying to stand atop a mound of melting wax. Bogged down in the swirling mass, he saw Angelica approaching him out of the corner of his eye. Enraged, he turned toward her, still struggling to free himself from his earthen snare.

"Please, Erik," she pleaded anxiously, "stop fighting it. The more that you fight, the quicker you'll sink!"

Erik was beyond all reason. He thrashed about, flailing his arms over and over again into the sifting soil in a primitive exercise in futility. The more he grappled, the faster the ground beneath his feet swallowed him up. Angelica stepped forward, desperately wanting to help him, but Erik's violent behavior prevented her from getting too close.Instead, she watched, as she had almost two years ago when she had defeated the Hellhound, as the demon that she called her friend sank down and away into the earth. When it was over, all that remained were the deep gouges in the dirt that Erik had made as he tried to pull himself free.

Slowly, Angelica walked over to the spot where Erik once stood. She stared at the ground – looking at it, but not really seeing it – saddened that it had ended this way, but gratified that the confrontation was finally over. She never wanted any part of this. She and Zoe had been the lone voices of dissent, but once Erik had begun the attack there was nothing left for them to do but fight.

She knelt down and placed a trembling hand upon the ground. Her head was tilted slightly and her eyes were closed, as though she were listening for something. The soft granules of soil beneath her fingertips, just clumps of dirt to others, sang out to her in a chorus of light and color. Images from far below the surface swam across the canopy of her consciousness as she searched the endless sea of earth for her friend. Angelica pushed with her mind, her thoughts reaching out like radar in an effort to locate Erik, but there was no response.

She took a deep breath and then opened her eyes. Angelica scooped up a handful of the sandy soil and stood up once more. The loose dirt slipped between her fingers and fell back to the ground, and all the while she stared at it curiously. She found it incredibly odd that she could not find Erik under the surface. It was highly unlikely that a creature the size and weight of Erik while in his demonic form could sink so far away so quickly that she could not detect its presence. Frustrated, she stared at the dirt that caked her palm, glanced at Erik's last known location one more time, and then began to make her way to the tree line with the hope of finding the others.

Her foot had barely left the ground when the earth beneath her feet screamed out to her like an alarm. Too late, she looked on in horror as the clearing seemed to explode all around her and she went soaring into the air. The wind howled in her ears and buffeted her face with such intensity that she found it difficult to breathe. She turned away from the turbulent force and gasped as her cheek brushed up against a leathery hide.

Angelica's ears popped and she winced at the pain, and when she finally opened her eyes she saw the world growing smaller and smaller beneath her. Large, heavy wings flapped up and down, assailing the air as they carried her even higher into the midday Michigan sky. Their apex reached, Erik stopped and hovered in mid-air. With his hand firmly about her waist, he held her out and away from him, staring at her with icy yellow-gold eyes.

"Yield," he said gruffly.

Angelica struggled for a bit within his rigid grasp and then eyed him furiously. "Stop this, Erik! You know that I am terrified of heights!"

"This ends," he growled as he squeezed her a tad bit tighter, "when you admit defeat."

Angelica dared to look below one more time and nearly passed out from fright. She took several deep breaths and looked at Erik fearfully. "What do you want from me?!" she pleaded.

"I want to hear you say it," he growled. He pulled her close, his eyes boring into her. Her eyes went wide with

17

fear, so much so that he began to regret having frightened her this way; but soon he realized that it was not him that she feared, but something else entirely. He was about to question her when a ball of flame slammed into his back. Taken completely by surprise, he turned to face the onslaught, only to be met by an even larger one straight to the chest. Momentarily stunned, his natural instinct was to protect himself, but in so doing he released his grip on Angelica and she fell, screaming, back to earth.

He glanced briefly at Blair as she hovered several feet above him, and deftly dodged the third fireball that she launched at him. The fact that her teammate was falling from the sky seemed of little consequence to her as she continued to lob the fiery orbs at him. Erik realized that Angelica's fate now rested solely in his hands. He pulled his wings in against his back, and leaning backward, fell out of the sky toward the ground.

He could sense Blair racing after him, but he paid little attention to her. Arcing his body, he angled himself into a position that propelled him through the sky toward Angelica like a missile shot. The speed at which he sailed through the air caused his eyes to well, but within seconds he had caught up with her. He scooped her up, cradling her in his arms, and then repositioned himself so that his back was now facing downward while she laid across his chest.

"Angelica!" he shouted over her hysterical screams. He held onto her tightly as she kicked and thrashed about in his arms. "Listen to me, Angelica, or we won't survive!"

She finally grew silent as they hurtled toward the ground. He could tell that she was beginning to hyperventilate. Her fear was so intense that she was digging her nails into his chest. He needed her to stay with him, in the moment, or they would both die.

"We are about to hit the ground and we are traveling too fast for me to open up my wings," he yelled quickly. "I need you to concentrate! I need you to provide us with a surface that I can hit without..." Erik began, but he quickly realized that it was too late.

He observed the tops of trees as they flashed past him, and within seconds they smacked into the center of the clearing. There was no resounding crash, however; instead, there was a loud *THUMP* as an immense cloud of dust was dispersed throughout the valley. For nearly a minute there was no movement, but as the haze began to clear, Angelica could be seen slowly climbing out of the large crater Erik's impact had created. She teetered haphazardly near the edge of the depression before regaining her senses, as well as her footing. She looked around at the damage done to the clearing, and then stared down angrily into the crater.

"I hope that hurt, you jerk!" she said bitterly.

"You have," Erik huffed roughly as he pulled himself painfully out of the crater, "no idea..." As he climbed over the edge he watched as Blair landed not too far from them. He regarded her warily as she approached them, and there was no mistaking the look in her eyes.

"You know that old saying 'turn that frown upside down?'" he joked as he stared at her angry features. "Well, it doesn't seem to be working for some people right about now."

Blair stopped and stood above the demon, her eyes locked on his. "Do you give up?" she asked, her tone hostile.

"You're joking, right?" Erik asked half-heartedly. "I just climbed up out of a hole in the ground – a hole that I made with my own body, I might add – my wings ache, I can't feel my legs, and I may have broken a nail. Are you seriously asking me if I surrender?!"

Blair raised her arms above her head and formed another massive fireball. "I won't ask again, Erik!" she said gruffly.

"I think that we have all seen enough," Tanna said as she exited the tree line, followed closely by Zoe, Eryn, and Annalise. A few moments later, Ian walked out of the trees, as well. He moved slowly, as though he were in pain; a slight limp hampering his movements as he made his way toward the crater.

"You said that the exercise wasn't over until one side surrendered," Blair said through gritted teeth. She never took her eyes off of Erik. The large, chaotic ball of fire that she had formed spun slowly above her head. "He started it – I plan on finishing it!"

"I said no such thing!" Tanna declared. The look that she saw in Blair's eyes chilled her to the bone, prompting her to place herself between Erik and the volatile Elemental. Tanna had grown more and more concerned about the girl's dark mood swings since their return from Avalon several months ago. Episodes like this one were now becoming more commonplace, and it truly worried her. "If you recall, I was firmly against this brutish...rehearsal, for lack of a better word. I found the entire display disgusting!" she fumed as she looked over her shoulder at Ian.

"Yes, yes, yes...," Ian said as he coughed raspily, "your complaints are duly noted, Tanna!" There was a wheeziness to his voice, as though he were having a hard time breathing. He made his way over to them and threw some clothes onto the demon's chest.

"Thank you," Erik growled. "Now if I could have a little privacy..."

Ian and Tanna both looked over at Blair, who was still standing over Erik with the swirling ball of fire suspended over her head. She glanced at the two of them from the corner of her eye and then sighed loudly. "Fine!" she exclaimed as the burning sphere winked out of existence. She turned on her heel and stormed off in a huff.

As Erik slid back down into the crater to begin his transformation, Tanna turned her attention back to Ian. She was still very much upset with her old friend, and she meant to tell him so, but her words came up short when she took in his appearance. His hair looked lifeless and brittle, and it hung loosely about his face. His eyes were glassy and bloodshot, and his cheeks seemed gaunt. His skin was pale and clammy to the touch,rendering the image of the exuberant and puckish rogue that she was familiar with to that of a frail and exhausted old man. Tanna took hold of Ian's arm and leaned in close to him.

"Are you all right?" she whispered as she eyed him worriedly.

"I admit that I'm feeling a little off my feet," Ian said smiling weakly just before another wave of dry, husky coughing came on. It took him a moment to overcome the gravely hacking. "It's nothing – most likely a bug. I'll be fine."

"You do not look fine," she said, concerned.

"I told you," Ian barked as he pushed past Tanna, "it's nothing!" He hobbled awkwardly over to the girls, stopped, and then motioned for her to join him. "Well," he snapped, "are you coming or not?!"

"What's wrong with him?" Erik asked as he walked up alongside Tanna. Now in his human form, he was buttoning up the shirt that Ian had brought for him.

"I suppose that we will find out when he decides to tell us," Tanna said as she turned to Erik. "Come, let's not keep him waiting."

Ian walked over to the girls and studied each of them individually. Inwardly, he was more than aware that none of them were the slightest bit happy with him at the moment, and if he were trying to win over their hearts and minds he would have understood completely. Unfortunately, he was here to protect them. It was his job to teach them how to protect themselves; and if that meant that they would grow to resent him, then so be it.

"Well ladies," he said pointedly as he approached the Elementals, "Tanna has already made me aware of her feelings as they relate to today's training. Do any of you wish to chime in?"

"Chime in...?" Eryn asked.

"Yes, yes," Ian said with a sigh. "Do any of you wish to tell me how unfair I'm being? Does anyone feel ill-used by mean old Ian?" he mocked.

The girls all looked at one another but remained silent. They had grown accustomed to this, it was Ian's way of weeding out the whiners. Once he was able to pinpoint one, he would deride them unmercifully – telling the others that it was all for their own good and that when the time came they would thank him one day.

24

"I have a question," Blair said as she faced the wizard. The other girls looked at her with stunned expressions and then turned their attention to Ian, eager for his response.

"Well then," he said as he watched Tanna and Erik walk up alongside the Elementals, "what is it? Don't leave me in suspense..."

"What's the point of all of this? Blair asked; her irritation plain for all to see. "We've defeated the Shadow King. Elwyn has been locked away, and all of his followers have been dealt with by Lathos; so...what's the point?"

"So," Ian said as he stared at Blair mockingly, "you believe that because all is well and good in the land of Avalon that you are safe?"

"Why shouldn't we?" Annalise demanded. "After all, you're the one who told us that everything was going to be fine now that the Shadow King has been exposed. What could you possibly be training us to face now?"

"We've been training like this for weeks," Blair continued, "for *weeks*! You haven't allowed any of us to return to Avalon, you won't explain why you're working us like this – something's going on and you're keeping us in the dark! Why?"

"I'm well aware of the fact that some of you are chomping at the bit to return to see your loved ones," Ian began.

"Speak for yourself," Eryn said, her tone terse. "My family is right here in Michigan!"

"I *did* say some of you," Ian continued as he waved his hand dismissively. "I assure you, once I have received word that everything is all in order you will be able to go to Avalon as often as you wish. Until then..."

Ian stopped talking as a small radio that he had in his breast pocket let loose with a stream of static. He placed a small earbud into his ear and listened intently to the chatter coming over the airwaves. Erik stepped up to him; his curiosity peaked as he watched his mentor's changing facial expressions.

"What's going on?" Erik asked. "What are you listening to?"

Ian motioned for silence and then concentrated on the radio for a few moments longer. Finally, he glanced up at Erik with a grim look in his eye. "It's a scanner, Master Hedley. I have taken to monitoring the local police bands while we conduct our training sessions. It seems that today's activities have garnered a bit of attention."

"What kind of attention?" Tanna asked anxiously.

"From what I can tell," Ian answered, "there seems to be a lot of traffic concerning what appears to be ball lightning and a rather large winged creature flying within the vicinity."

"What are you saying?" Eryn asked. "Is someone coming out to the island?"

"Quite a few someones," Ian replied, "from what I can gather."

"Sounds like it's time to go," Erik said.

"My thoughts exactly," Tanna agreed. "How much time do we have before they arrive,Ian?"

"Five, possibly ten minutes," Ian said before another fit of coughing took him.

Tanna studied her old friend. His worsening condition was truly beginning to unsettle her. "Erik," she said as she kept a watchful eye on Ian, "could you provide us with a portal to my home? We can continue this discussion there."

"Not a problem," Erik said confidently, "but you'll have to count me out. I have to get home. My dad has been acting kinda strange lately, what with all of the time that I have been spending with you guys."

"I shan't be joining you, either," Ian said, his coughing spell diminishing. "I will be returning to the Kensington for a bit of a lie-down…"

"Ian, I really think that…," Tanna began, but she stopped when she saw the look in his eye.

"So," Erik said, "we need three separate portals for three different destinations? Piece of cake!"

"Since when," Zoe asked skeptically, "have you been able to form more than one stable portal at a time? I don't think I have ever seen *Ian* attempt anything like that!"

Erik threw his girlfriend a wink. "You mean that you have never seen anything like *this*?" he asked with a wily smile. He waved his hand in the air and within seconds three portals appeared behind him. "The one on the left goes to Tanna's, the one in the middle goes to the Kensington, and the last one is for me!"

"Erik," Tanna exclaimed, "that is incredible! How did you do that?"

"There will be plenty of time for the boy to regale us with his ever-growing skills in magic," Ian interrupted before Erik could answer, "suffice it to say the portals are here. I suggest we use them with all due haste!"

*   *   *

Erik emerged from the portal deep within a row of cherry trees. It was nearing the end of the harvest season, and all of the trees' succulent red fruit had been nearly plucked and collected. A few of the branches still held tightly to their treasure, but those stragglers would eventually fall to the ground; aiding Mother Nature with her ever-revolving circle of life. Erik reached up and grabbed a handful of the tiny crimson fruit and popped some into his mouth. He exited the orchard and made his way up toward his family's home; his hopes of getting something more substantial to eat dashed as the sound of someone pounding on a window in a nearby outbuilding intruded upon his thoughts.

Erik looked over at the structure that was used by the foreman as an office and saw his father waving wildly at him. It was obvious that the man wanted to speak with him, and Erik took several seconds to weigh his options. Realizing, at last, that ignoring his father and continuing on to the house would only infuriate him further, Erik stuffed his hands into his pockets and walked begrudgingly over to the office.

Stepping into the building, Erik nodded his head in greeting to Dan Henderson. Dan had worked for his family for as long as Erik could remember. Dan's father had been foreman before him, and he was extremely proud of having obtained the position himself through hard work and sacrifice – not because it was *his turn*. Dan smiled at Erik as the boy tossed him a cherry, but the expression fell off of the man's face when Junior Hedley began to tear into him again.

"I want you to know why I called my son in here, Dan." Junior fumed as he glared at his foreman. "All of this is going to be his one day," he said before turning his gaze toward Erik, "that is if he ever decides to put his nose to the grindstone instead of chasing after skirts!"

"I'm not chasing after...," Erik tried to say, but his father waved him off.

"Do you *like* your job, Dan?" Junior asked, ignoring his son.

"Yes sir, Mr. Hedley." Dan answered.

"You do, do you?" Junior growled. "Well, I don't believe you. I'm looking at the numbers for this year's harvest, Dan; and I am having a hard time believing that you like your job!"

"Dad," Erik tried to say in Dan's defense, "Dan is one of the hardest working..."

"Quit interrupting, boy!" Junior said angrily. "I'm trying to teach you an important lesson in business management!"

Junior turned his back on his son and returned his attention to his foreman. Erik lurched toward his father; menace in his eyes, his brow furrowed and his cheeks hot with anger. He stopped himself from reaching out and grabbing Junior by the throat – an act that was sorely desired by the one within him – and took a seat in the corner of the room instead. His nostrils flared and his hands were shaking. It took several deep breaths to finally quell the rage that had been building up inside him.

"I walk the orchards and do you know what I see, Dan?" Jr continued, completely unaware of what his son had almost done.

"Cherries," Dan murmured.

"What was that, Dan? I didn't quite hear you."

"Cherries," Dan said a bit louder this time.

"Darn skippy!" Junior yelled. "Cherries! But not just cherries, Dan. That's money. Money still sitting in my trees and they're going to waste! Money that should be going into my bank account. Am I right?!"

"Yes sir," Dan answered.

"Of course, I am!" Junior stated cruelly as he walked over to Erik and took a seat beside him. He failed to notice the beads of sweat on his son's forehead. "So," he went on, "what's the reason for all of that money still sitting in those trees, Dan? Please, enlighten me!"

Dan shuffled his feet nervously and peered red-faced about the room. He glanced out the window for a moment, as though he were looking for salvation from outside the spartan little office, and then gathered his thoughts before he answered Junior.

"The workers are afraid, sir." he said, his voice quivering.

"Afraid of what?" Junior asked brusquely.

Dan hesitated, and then he screwed up his courage. "They're afraid of the Terror, sir." he said as he maintained eye contact with his boss.

"The...*what?*" Junior asked dubiously.

"The Traverse City Terror," Dan said again. "At least that's what everyone is calling it. They've all been talking about it. Surely you've heard other people talking about it, sir? Erik?"

Junior tore his eyes away from Dan and looked over at his son. "Do you have *any* idea what he is talking about?"

Erik shrugged his shoulders and tried not to look directly at Dan. "Nope – never heard of it before."

"C'mon guys," Dan said, becoming more animated as he took several steps toward them, "you haven't heard the stories about the giant creature that's been sighted around this area? The thing's supposed to be at least twenty feet tall, with giant golden horns on its head. It's got wings a mile long and razor sharp fangs that drip acid! They say that it flies around the TC looking for unwary victims to take back to its den, where it eats them whole! You're honestly going to tell me that neither one of you have heard about the Terror?!"

Erik and Junior stared at Dan with eyes wide with shock; their mouths hanging open in surprise and disbelief. While Junior could not believe that there were people actually walking about spreading this nonsense, Erik was stunned to find out that such an image had been painted of him. It was bad enough to learn that he had been seen so often that a nearly accurate description of the demon was floating around – but *eating* people!

"Dan," Junior said slowly, "please tell me that you do not believe any of this."

"I, uh...," Dan said as his cheeks flushed red in embarrassment, "...no sir. *I* don't believe one word of it, but the workers – some of them claim to have seen the creature, sir!"

"The only *creature* with *wings* that any of those losers might have seen," Junior snarled, "is on the label of the bottle of hootch that they pass around when they think that I'm not paying attention!" Junior got to his feet and stormed over to Dan, his finger pointed squarely in the other man's face. "Now you listen to me – I don't care what you do to get those jokers back to work, but you do it and you do it NOW! Is that clear?"

"Yes sir, Mr. Hedley!" Dan said. He took one last look at Erik, and then turned and walked out the door.

"I would not have believed it had I not heard it with my own ears!" Junior scoffed. He shook his head and, as though it were an afterthought, turned his attention to Erik. "Nice to see that you remembered where you live by the way. Where have you been all day?"

"Just out," Erik said casually, "you know – hanging with Zoe."

"*Just hanging with Zoe*," Junior said sarcastically. "I swear boy, you would think that girl had a ring looped through your nose!"

"I like spending time with her," Erik said with a scowl. "What's wrong with that?"

"What's wrong with it," Junior snapped, "is that you aren't focusing on the future! *You're* future! This orchard is going to be yours one day, and I don't want it falling to crap because you're out following some girl like a love sick puppy!"

Erik did not need to hear another word. He had learned long ago to shut his father out when he started behaving this way. He climbed out of his chair and made his way toward the door. "I'm out of here," he said.

"I want you to start spending more time with Dan," Junior insisted as he slapped a meaty hand onto Erik's shoulder. When his son turned and faced him he was amazed at the realization that they were now the same height. *When did that happen?* he thought to himself.

"You need to understand how this place operates," Junior continued. "I would show you myself, but I have more important things to do. Dan can show you the ropes; maybe it will give you some purpose to your life."

Erik glanced at his father's hand on his shoulder. "Whatever," he sneered as he shrugged off his father's grip.

"Look, boy," Junior said as Erik reached for the door knob, "I know what you're going through, believe me. It's great having a girlfriend, but a girlfriend can't put food on the table." Junior stopped and thought for a moment, and then smiled stupidly. "Then again, when you stop and think about it, they *do* put food on the table, don't they?" Junior began laughing at his own joke.

"That wasn't funny," Erik said under his breath.

"Oh lighten up, boy!" Junior said with a snide look on his face. "It was just a joke. When did you become such a wuss?"

Erik turned and faced his father. He took a step toward Junior and looked him straight in the eye. "That," he growled, "was *not* funny!"

Junior was taken aback by the look in his son's eyes. There was a quality about them that chilled Junior right down to the bone. He vaguely recalled feeling this way at his own father's house some time ago, but when he tried to piece together the images that this feeling invoked, all he got was a hazy cloud. What he did remember, and clearly, was the fear – it was the same gut-wrenching fear that he was experiencing right now.

"O-okay, boy!" he stammered. "I didn't mean anything by it. I-it was a stupid joke. I'm sorry!"

Erik was so close to his father that their noses nearly touched. He stared icily at Junior for a moment more after the lame apology had left the man's lips, and then he turned and left the building. Junior slumped backward and fell against the desk; his heart racing at an alarming rate.

For a moment – a brief moment – Junior honestly felt as if his life had been in danger, but this was his son! Surely *he* would never have the nerve to stand up to him. No one, absolutely no one, stood up to Junior; at least that was what he kept telling himself. Junior had been involved in more than a few situations in his day that could have ended badly, and he had met them all head on – that is until now. He had just witnessed something that would forever haunt his dreams; something that he would deny if anyone ever asked him of it. When his son had confronted him, stood up to him for the first time in his life, Junior could have sworn that his son's eyes had begun to glow. They burned the brightest yellow-gold that Junior had ever seen, and it had nearly scared him to death.

2. An Informal Gathering

Morgan le Fay regarded the edifice that housed the Traverse City Police department as a spider would a fly – a fateful smile working its way slowly across her lips. She walked up the short flight of stairs and approached the set of glass doors that displayed the TCPD logo. Morgan gasped as the partitions separated of their own accord; the advance of manmade technology impressing her once again. She stepped into the air conditioned building and made her way past photographs of police officers, sports and marksmanship trophies, wanted posters and other miscellaneous bulletins and walked over to the desk that was manned by a lone police officer.

She stood at the counter quietly as the desk sergeant spoke to someone on the telephone. He looked up at her and grinned apologetically, motioning to the phone. She did not return his smile; instead, she bent over and read the name tag that was over his right breast pocket.

"I must speak with Chief Whipple, Sergeant Ryan. Can you tell me if he is still in charge of this facility?"

"I'll be with you in just a minute," Sergeant Ryan said, still smiling as he placed his hand over the mouthpiece of the telephone. Morgan scowled irritably, her work here was of great importance to her and she had neither the time nor the inclination to be put off.

"I asked you a question," she said with an indignant tone. "Is Chief Whipple here or not?!"

The officer, clearly annoyed, placed his hand over the mouthpiece once again. "And *I* asked *you* to be a little patient! I'll be right with you."

"How *dare* you!" Morgan said, seething. She reached across the desk and placed her index finger onto his forehead. Sergeant Ryan instantly looked up at her, his phone conversation forgotten.

"I'm sorry, my lady; how can I assist you?" the police officer asked with a silvery voice.

"Now that is more like it," Morgan smiled. She watched as the police officer let the phone fall to the floor. He then came around the desk, took her hand, and stared lovingly into her eyes. "I am looking for Chief Whipple," she asked again. "Is he in?"

"Chief Whipple?" the desk sergeant repeated, somewhat disappointed. "Why yes, he's here. I believe that he is in his office, but..." he hesitated for just a moment,

"...but couldn't I help you? I happen to be the 'go to' guy around here. Whatever you need, I'm your man!"

"I do appreciate the offer," Morgan said smiling sweetly, "but the Chief and I are old acquaintances. However, I will definitely keep you in mind should the need arise!"

"Thank you, dear lady, thank you!" Sergeant Ryan said as he kissed her hand. "If you go down that hallway and turn right, you will find Chief Whipple's office. His is the second door on your left."

"Thank you once again, Sergeant Ryan." Morgan gave him a weak smile as she pulled her hand from his grasp. She waltzed past the befuddled policeman and made her way down the hall as directed. As she disappeared into the corridor, Sergeant Ryan shook his head groggily. For a moment he had no idea where he was. Seeing the phone lying on the floor, he bent over, picked it up, and placed it to his ear. Upon hearing a busy signal, he simply shrugged his shoulders and placed the handset back onto its cradle. He sat back down at his desk and continued on with his paperwork.

Morgan glided down the hallway, following Sergeant Ryan's directions, until she came to the door marked 'Police

Chief.' She entered the room and smiled when she saw Chief Whipple, his back to her, going through a filing cabinet. Not wanting to startle him, she coughed lightly to get his attention. The Chief turned around and stared at her curiously.

"Hello!" he said, surprised that no one had informed him that there was someone here to see him. "Can I help you, ma'am?"

"I knew that my magic was strong," Morgan said as she clapped her hands gleefully, "but could it truly be possible that you are still in my thrall even after all of this time?"

"I...I don't understand," Chief Whipple said confused. "Do...do I *know* you?"

"Of course you know me," Morgan said with an icy tone to her voice. "It is I – Morgan! Morgan le Fay!"

Chief Whipple stared at her. "*You're* Morgan le Fay? *The* Morgan le Fay?"

"Who else would I be?!" Morgan replied exasperated. She held her arms up on either side and twirled around so he could get a good look at her. "Do you not recognize me?"

"Lady," Chief Whipple said with a chuckle, "I'm sure that this is all some sort of elaborate joke – more than likely something that Ryan or one of the others cooked up; but I really don't have time for fun and games, unfortunately. I've got a lot of work to do..."

"You think that this is all part of some 'elaborate joke'?!" Morgan bristled. "I assure you; this is *no* joke!"

"Look, ma'am," Chief Whipple said kindly, "I can appreciate a good laugh just as much as the next guy, but I really am very busy. If you would like, I can walk you back to the front desk. We can both tell Sergeant Ryan that we had a good laugh and..."

Chief Whipple abruptly froze in place as Morgan took possession of his mind. Her eyes became jet black and the room grew cold, as inky black tendrils of mist swirled all around the hapless police chief. The smoky tentacles attempted to enter Whipple's body, attacking him from all sides, but the murky coils seemed to flinch away from him as though they were in pain.

Morgan was at a loss. There was no way that a mere mortal could have developed the ability to thwart her enticements, and yet... Curious, she approached him and looked into his eyes. She hissed angrily when she saw his pupils; for in them, she found the answer to her question. As she glared at Chief Whipple she could see her own reflection in his silver-hued pupils.

"Someone has placed a blocking spell upon you," she said outraged. "I demand to know who has done this to you, and why!"

"He was afraid that you might return one day," Chief Whipple said slowly, as though in a trance. "He wanted to make sure that you could never use any of us ever again."

"He?" Morgan spat. "To whom are you referring?"

"Ian," Chief Whipple answered. "Ian Rimmel."

"Ian Rimmel?!" Morgan barked. "Was he not the miserable little upstart I sent you after when I was here last?"

"Yes," Chief Whipple responded. "He was afraid that you might return one day..."

"You do not have to tell me again," Morgan growled angrily. "I heard you the first time!" She waved her hand in front of the policeman's face and watched as his eyes returned to their normal color. The hazy fingers of vapor quickly vanished and everything about the office returned to normal.

"I...I'm sorry," the police chief said, sounding confused, as he looked about the room curiously, "I got a little dizzy there for a second!" He watched as Morgan paced irritably back and forth. "What was I saying...?"

"You were telling me all about a man that I desperately need to locate," Morgan said without looking at him. He may have become useless as a slave, but perhaps he could be helpful in another capacity. "You were offering to help me find him!"

"I was offering to help you find someone?" Chief Whipple asked. "Who?"

"His name," Morgan said as she finally turned and faced him, "is Ian Rimmel."

"I can't say that I ever heard of anyone by that name," Chief Whipple said shaking his head, "and I'm pretty sure that I did not agree to help you find him." He held up a stack of papers and waved them in her face. "Do you see this? Do you?! Read my lips: I'm too busy! The mayor's breathing down my neck for this budget report — and why am I even explaining any of this to you?

"A strange woman comes barging into my office," he went on as he stared into Morgan's hate-filled eyes, "claiming to be some magic wizard-lady from out of a fairy tale; and now I'm supposed to drop everything and help you find someone I've never heard of? I don't mean to sound rude, but it ain't happening, lady!"

"But you must help me!" Morgan whined. "It is imperative that I locate him immediately!"

"And it's imperative that I get my work done!" Chief Whipple said, exasperated. "Look, I am more than willing…," he stopped as he caught a glimpse of something in the hallway outside his office. "Hey, you two," he yelled desperately, "come in here for a minute!"

Immediately on guard, Morgan turned and eyed the two police officers that stepped into the office behind her warily. She quickly took account of them both; the one on her left had a playful look about him – as though he tried not to take the world much too seriously. The one to her right was the polar opposite. He took in the entire room and its occupants with several swipes of his eyes. His demeanor was no nonsense; wound tightly, he appeared ready for trouble. She had no doubt that he would be quick to clamp down on any foolishness at the first sign of it.

"Gentlemen," Chief Whipple said, "This is…Morgan. Morgan, this is Captain Eagler and Captain Sims."

"Ma'am," the officers said in way of a greeting.

"Morgan here has a problem." *And that's putting it mildly,* Chief Whipple thought to himself before going on. "It seems that she is desperate to find someone who may be here in Traverse City. If your plates aren't full, do you two think that you could give her a hand in locating this guy?"

The two men glanced at each other before answering. "I'm good," Captain Sims said.

"I'd be happy to help," Captain Eagler echoed.

"Well...uh...Morgan," Chief Whipple said, happy to have pawned her off onto someone else, "is it okay if these two officers help you out?"

"Yes," Morgan purred, smiling as she approached the two men, "they will do nicely!"

*   *   *

Tanna and the girls returned home that afternoon directly from the training site. Angelica asked if everyone could stay for dinner, and after receiving the thumbs up from her grandmother, and then several phone calls for permission from the other parents, they set about with the preparations. Tanna removed the cover from the barbecue grill and started up the propane burners while Angelica went inside for hamburgers and hotdogs. Annalise and Zoe helped prepare the salad, Blair located several cans of baked beans, and Eryn gathered the sandwich buns and condiments. Once everything was ready, they gathered at the patio table, took their seats, and dug in.

Their dinner conversation was light-hearted and filled with laughter, and it pleased Tanna greatly to hear the girls talking about the things that generally encompassed the lives of fifteen and sixteen-year-old girls. The strain of keeping secrets from their families, the grueling training sessions with Erik and Ian, and the fact that they had been forbidden from returning to Avalon – all of that seemed miles away as their playful joking and friendly banter made Tanna laugh, as well.

With dinner finished, they were just beginning to clean up the dishes when Erik rode into the backyard on his bike. Zoe went over to greet him as he leaned the mountain bike against the shed. She could see the troubled look in his eyes, and they spoke quietly for a moment before joining the others. Erik plopped down into one of the empty chairs at the table, declining to eat the last hamburger that was offered to him.

"Erik Hedley turning down food," Eryn said feigning shock, "now I've seen everything!"

"His dad has been hassling him again," Zoe said as she took his hand in hers.

Tanna became concerned. "Is there a problem, Erik?"

"Not really," Erik said as he gave Zoe's hand a squeeze. "He just thinks that I am spending way too much time with you guys." He turned to Zoe and grinned sheepishly. "You, in particular."

"You can't help it if you have good taste," Zoe teased.

"He also wants me to start hanging out with our foreman," Erik said to Tanna. "He thinks that I need to start learning how the orchard operates."

"And what do *you* think?" she asked him.

"I don't know," Erik grumbled. "I've got other things on my mind right now."

"What kind of things?" Annalise asked curiously.

"Things like the farm hands at the orchard noticing strange chemical smells in the air. Some are saying that they have seen what looks like a 'doorway to another dimension,' but it disappears before they can get near it."

"The portals," Blair whispered.

"Yeah," Erik said. "Oh, and the *best* one – they are all afraid of this large creature that has been sighted flying around the orchard at night looking for people to eat!"

"They've seen you in your demon form?!" Annalise asked, shocked.

"No," Erik said quickly. "They're not sure *what* they've see. I'm sure that no one has actually seen the creature well enough to actually come forward with a description."

"Well, *that's* comforting...," Angelica said sarcastically.

"You must be more careful, Erik!" Tanna scolded him.

"I know! I know! That's why I rode my bike all the way over here instead of using a portal!"

"Wow," Eryn said, "I can only imagine what Ian will say when he hears about all of this!"

"That," Erik grumbled, "is the one thing that I am trying *not* to think about!"

"Speaking of Ian," Angelica said as they all turned to face her, "has anyone else noticed that he hasn't quite been himself lately?"

"He did look a little out of it," Blair acknowledged, "what with all of the coughing and hacking."

Annalise looked fixedly at Tanna. "He *is* all right, isn't he?" she asked concerned.

"There is no need to fret," Tanna lied. "I, too, was worried about him; but he told me that everything was fine."

"And you believed him...?" Annalise said with a smirk.

"I'm positive that once he has had some time to rest," Tanna said reassuringly, "that he will be back to his old tricks!"

Without warning, and as if on cue, a portal opened up in Tanna's backyard. She smiled, relieved that her old friend had indeed gotten better and was now returning to visit them. Tanna stood up and turned to the others as a form began to coalesce out of the milky cloudiness of the rift.

"There, you see!" she said with a grin. "It's just as I said. He just needed a little rest!"

Tanna made her way toward the portal but stopped in her tracks when she laid eyes upon the rift's occupant. He was a bit disheveled; his hair and clothing a mess, with a slight growth of stubble on his face. He stumbled out of the portal and shielded his eyes from the sun's light. He tried to obscure his features, but there was no mistaking the man standing before her. Stunned, her voice caught in her throat; but soon, she composed herself enough to finally say his name.

"Elwyn...?!" she whispered.

"No! Th-that's impossible!" Blair said shocked, as she watched her brother step out of the portal. "You're supposed to be locked away!"

Before the Sidhe prince could answer her, Erik had bounded across the yard – fully transformed – and hefted the young heir to the throne of Gorias off of his feet. He slammed the prince onto the ground, his massive hand wrapped around Elwyn's throat, and pushed his face down into the dirt.

"Give me *one* good reason why I shouldn't break your neck!" Erik roared.

"Because he is with me," a voice called out from behind him. Erik turned his head, his mouth agape, as someone else exited the portal. "Believe it or not, *this time,* he is on our side!"

Averyil stepped out of the portal, and as she did, the rift closed up behind her. Her appearance was similar to that of Elwyn's. Her hair, while unkempt, was pulled back into a ponytail. Her face was smudged with dirt and what looked like dried blood; and her left arm was wrapped in a bandage that had been thrown on in a slapdash fashion, as though there had been no time to apply it properly. She carried her trusty staff firmly in her other hand, and there was something sticky and wet on one of its blunted ends.

"Ohmagosh!" Zoe exclaimed as she and Annalise rushed over to their sister. The three girls embraced each other warmly, and then regretfully, Averyil turned her attention back to Erik.

"Please Erik," she asked again, "release him. I can explain everything."

"You're telling me that this piece of garbage is one of the good guys now?" Erik growled.

"It is nice to see you again, too!" Elwyn mumbled, his mouth full of dirt.

"What I am saying," Averyil said as she glared at Elwyn, "is that we are to trust him. For now..."

Erik snorted in discontent before releasing his grip on Elwyn. The prince got to his feet slowly and brushed the dirt and debris from his clothing. He massaged his neck a bit before extending his hand out to the demon that stood glaring over him.

"Here is to putting the past behind us," Elwyn said hopefully.

"I *will* find a reason to hurt you!" Erik murmured before he turned his back on the Sidhe. He glanced at Tanna, shrugging his immense shoulders awkwardly. "You wouldn't happen to have anything that I could put on, would you?"

"As it so happens," she said with a knowing grin, "Ian and I discussed being prepared for just such an event." She looked over at Angelica. "Could you run into the guest room and get clothes and shoes for Erik, please?"

"You got it!" Angelica said as she morphed into her Sidhe form and zipped into the house. Within seconds, she had returned and handed Erik his garments.

"Thank you," he mumbled as he went off behind the shed to transform and put on his clothing.

Elwyn looked at everyone in the backyard and smiled pleasantly. "I must admit that you all do make for rather attractive looking humans," and then under his breath, he said, "if there is such a thing."

"We look like this so we can protect our secret," Blair answered gruffly, "and our families!"

"I completely understand," Elwyn said as he walked toward her with open arms. "And speaking of family, do you not have a hug for your big brother?"

"How did you get here?" Blair asked Averyil; completely ignoring Elwyn's remark. "You don't have the ability to open portals – do you?"

"I do not," Averyil answered. "Elwyn opened the rift that brought us here."

"That's impossible," Erik commented as he approached the group. He was back in his human form once again and was buttoning up his shirt. "There is no way that he could have opened up a portal here. He would have to have a frame of reference to be able to get to this realm. I doubt that he's ever been *here* before."

"You are correct," Elwyn said. "*I* do not know this realm, but *Merlin* does!"

Tanna eyed the prince skeptically. "You're telling us that Merlin gave *you* the information required to get here? Why would he do that?"

"Perhaps he thought that I would be a valuable asset in the coming war," Elwyn said casually.

"What war?" Annalise asked. "What are you talking about?"

"Things are not as you all remember them in Avalon," Averyil said. "Merlin began meeting with several of us shortly after your departure – including Elwyn. Once he realized the true nature of the Shadow King..."

"You mean Elwyn," Erik scoffed.

"No. I do not," Averyil said. "I believed Elwyn to be the Shadow King as well, but it would seem that we were all mistaken."

"Well, if Elwyn isn't the Shadow King," Eryn asked, "then who is?"

"Our dear brother," Elwyn said coolly as he glanced over at Blair, "Lathos. Lathos is the Shadow King."

Blair walked over to her brother and glared at him. "You. Are. A liar!"

"I am sorry, Blair; but Elwyn speaks the truth," Averyil said sadly.

Blair continued to stare angrily at her brother; the pain and fury evident in her eyes. Elwyn could see that she was hurting, and her distress affected him deeply.

"I know that I did terrible things," he said softly, "and for that, I am truly sorry. If it means anything, I want you to know that I was not responsible for any of my actions."

"What are you talking about?" Zoe asked angrily.

"I was bewitched," Elwyn said to her, "by one of Lathos' accomplices. A vile witch placed a spell over me. She tricked me into behaving the way that I did in order to deceive everyone and keep Lathos' secret safe."

"Avalon must be a breeding ground for evil witches!" Annalise spat. "They seem to be all over the place!"

"It doesn't matter," Blair said as her bottom lip trembled, "don't you see that? She may have manipulated you, but it would not have been possible if you didn't already have those feelings inside you to begin with!"

"That may be true," Elwyn acknowledged, "but all I ever sincerely desired was to make the Sidhe one people once again!"

"And now, thanks to you *and* Lathos, the Sidhe are in disarray and Alron is dead!" Blair said through gritted teeth. "I hate you both!"

"So," Tanna asked Averyil in a desperate attempt to change the subject, "why did Merlin send you here?"

"Merlin did not send us," she said slowly, "Merin is dead."

"What?!" Tanna exclaimed, her face cloaked in disbelief.

"It is true," Averyil said. "Once I received the news of the mage's death, my grandfather and I broke Elwyn out of prison and then we made our way here. I did not know what else to do!"

Tanna nodded her head distractedly as she contemplated her next move. She looked up, her face set and her course determined; once again the leader of their gathering. "I want you to save the rest of your account, Averyil. There is someone who needs to hear it from start to finish. Erik," she said as she placed a hand on his shoulder, "I need you to go and get Ian!"

*　　*　　*

Erik and Zoe stepped out of the fracture of time and space and into the gardens behind the Kensington. As the portal closed after them, they made their way to the front of the grand hotel. From the moment that he had arrived here, Ian had made the manor house turned hotel his home. He had cast a spell over the owner Hank, enabling him to come and go as he pleased without the old man having remembered that he had ever been there. Ian's room, large and grandiose – like his ego – could only be reached by placing one's hand along the wall next to the fireplace. Once the magic phrase was spoken, a door would appear on the wall; and within moments of entering the room, it would disappear again.

As they entered the lobby, they were confronted by Hank. He was waving his hand wildly, attempting to get their attention, while he held a mobile phone in the other. Erik and Zoe exchanged concerned glances as they listened in on his conversation.

"…that's right. I said Ian Rimmel," Hank said anxiously into the phone as he stopped the two teens from entering the main room. "No, I don't know who he is! I found him in my lobby babbling like an idiot…yes, he's still here. I truly can't see him going anywhere in his current condition!" Hank was quiet for a moment, and then a look of relief spread across his face. "You've been looking for him? Great! Then I'll see you in a bit. Thank you!"

Hank hung up the phone and looked at Erik and Zoe, "If you two are here for a bite to eat, I can't help you right now. There's some nut in the lobby – I can't tell if he's drunk or simply off his rocker. Who can tell these days?!"

"Did you say this guy's name is Ian Rimmel?" Erik asked worriedly.

"Yeah," Hank answered as he looked back into the lobby. "At least that's what he keeps saying. Why, does the name sound familiar to you?"

"He might be a friend of ours," Zoe said nervously. "Could we see him, please?"

Hank eyed the two for a moment before waving them into the lobby. As they approached one of the large sofas in the center of the room they could see Ian, clammy and pale, lying on his back. His hair was wet and pasted to his forehead, and he seemed to be unconscious. Erik rushed over to him and gently shook him, but all he got from his mentor was a muffled groan.

"Do you *know* this guy?" Hank asked.

"Yeah," Erik said as he helped lift Ian into a sitting position. "He's our friend. How did he get here?"

"Beats the heck out of me," Hank said as he looked the strange man over. "One minute I'm at the counter doing the bills, and the next thing I know he's lying on the couch talking to himself. It was like he appeared out of thin air!"

"You said that he was talking to himself," Zoe said to Hank. "What exactly was he saying?"

"Now that's something else that weirded me out," Hank said quickly. "Strangest thing I ever heard. He kept repeating 'I, Ian Rimmel, am the first and the last. The book shall be mine!' Now, what do you suppose he meant by that?"

"It's hard to say," Erik said as he stood Ian up, supporting him with his arm around the wizard's waist while Ian's arm was draped over Erik's shoulder. "But I'm sure that he will be okay once we get him home!"

"Whoa," Hank said as he put his hand out to stop Erik, "what do you mean? I can't let you leave with him. The police are on their way!"

"We have to get him home," Zoe said hurriedly. "His medicine is there – he's, uh, diabetic! He could be suffering from low blood sugar!"

"Really?" Hank said as he looked at Ian once again. "I don't know..."

"Hank," Erik pleaded, "we have to get him out of here!"

"Well...okay," Hank relented. "I'm glad you two got here when you did! Are you going to need any help getting him home?"

"No, my...uh...car is right out back," Erik lied. "We've got his. Thanks for keeping an eye on him, Hank!"

"Don't mention it," Hank said with a perplexed look on his face. "Let me know if there's anything I can do for you!" he yelled as he watched the three of them leave the lobby and exit the hotel.

"We will. Thanks again!" Zoe said as she waved at Hank, and then she ran out the door behind Erik and Ian.

Hank stood in the middle of the lobby for a moment, scratching his head. He still could not figure out how the strange man had come to be in his hotel; someone in that condition would have been far too noticeable to be able to slip inside without being seen. And how was it that the Hedley boy and his girlfriend knew such a character? As he walked back over to his desk another thought struck him — since when did Erik drive a car? Shrugging his shoulders, he sat down and went back to work on his bills.

He had only been sitting for a short while when a strange feeling came over him. The hair on the back of his neck stood on end and a shiver made its way down his spine. It was the oddest of sensations; it was as though he were being watched. He gripped the arms of his chair tightly as he slowly swiveled the seat around, and nearly screamed when he saw the two police officers standing there. They, too, had entered without making a sound or saying a word; their eyes hidden behind mirrored sunglasses and their hands clad in black leather gloves. The larger of the two men was leaning over the counter. Hank could see his own reflection in the lenses of the glasses, and he could feel the other man's eyes boring into him.

"You called our dispatch center," Captain Eagler said. It was not a question. "We're here for Mister Rimmel."

"M-mister who…?" Hank said, so rattled that he forget for a moment that he had placed the call.

"Rimmel," Captain Sims said with an unnatural looking smile on his face. "Ian Rimmel. You told the dispatcher that he was here. We've come to...take him someplace safe."

Hank looked back and forth at the two men; the warning bells inside his head ringing profusely. "Um...yeah, him...well, you see, uh, he...he must have left!"

Even with the dark glasses on, the scowl on Eagler's face was evident. "Are you telling us that the guy just up and left? You didn't try to stop him?"

"Well, I didn't see him leave, did I?" Hank said, sweating. "You can't expect me to sit here and stare at him until you arrive, can you?"

Eagler leaned in closer. "Listen to me, old man..."

"What my partner is trying to say," Sims said as he placed a hand of restraint on Eagler's shoulder, "is that you probably should have let our dispatch center know that he had left. Could you give us a description of him please?" Again, Captain Sims stared at him with his creepy smile.

Hank nodded his head numbly as he gave the police officers Ian's description. Neither of the men took notes; they just inclined their heads slightly as Hank told them all that they wanted to know. When he had finished, the officers looked at one another, nodded, and then turned to leave without a further word to Hank.

"I-is that all?" Hank asked nervously. "Do you guys need anything else from me?"

Eagler stopped and turned his head, looking at Hank from over his shoulder. "Why? Are you planning on leaving town?"

"Uh...no," Hank said timidly.

"Well then," Eagler said as he walked away, "if we need anything else from you we'll know exactly where to find you."

As the two men left the hotel, Hank fell back into his chair. His heart was beating a mile a minute, and his hands were trembling so badly that he had a hard time steadying them. Something had warned him not to mention Erik and Zoe to the policemen, and he was glad that he had not. There was something not quite right about them; something that Hank could not put his finger on, but whatever it was truly frightened him.

"I don't know what you kids have gotten yourselves into," he said aloud, "but you best sure get yourselves out of it!"

*   *   *

The reflection of the Blue moon, the second full moon that month, gleamed brightly in the calm still waters of Duck Lake. Usually awash in music from nearby Interlochen, tonight everything within the lake's periphery was being serenaded by the calling song of a multitude of male cicada. The sound created by their tymbols – the organs that enabled them to produce a call that was the loudest of any known insect – carried gently along by a cool nighttime breeze, only enhanced the mystical quality of the evening. A few yards away from the lake, nestled amongst some trees, a solitary cabin's light leaked out into the darkness as Eagler took one more look around. Finally satisfied that they were alone, he turned and rejoined Morgan le Fay and his partner Sims inside the cottage.

"You know," Sims said as he cleared away Morgan's dinner dishes, "there is such a thing as being overly cautious. We are completely – and totally – alone out here."

Eagler glared at the other officer; his large onyx-colored eyes piercing Sims' back scathingly. "You can never be too cautious – even you know that."

"What I know is that the campground is deserted," Sims said as he returned from the kitchen. "I made certain, when I found this place, that the Mistress would have the entire area to herself!"

Morgan stared silently out the window as the two men bantered back and forth. She drummed her fingernails on the sill, her frustration building as they continued to spar. Finally, her nerves frayed, she turned and silenced them both with a look.

"What of this Ian Rimmel?" she asked as Eagler and Sims grew quiet. "Would it not be a more beneficial use of your time if you focused your energies on locating him instead of squabbling like children?"

"The man's a ghost," Sims said quickly. "We hit every hotel, inn, and B and B within a twenty-mile radius. No one has heard of him, let alone seen anyone fitting his description."

"We've alerted night shift to be on the look out for him," Eagler said. "We will do the same thing tomorrow with first and second shift, as well."

"The man could not simply disappear!" Morgan barked. "I refuse to believe that he has slipped through my fingers again!"

"You mentioned dealing with him before to Chief Whipple," Sims said. "If I may ask, Mistress: who exactly *is* this guy?"

"If only I knew," Morgan said, vexed. Her eyes became as black as pitch as she swirled her fingers in the air. As she did so, letters made of flame appeared before her. She stepped back and stared at the fiery name that floated in front of her – IAN RIMMEL. Her face grew dark as she stared at the name of the mysterious man who had begun to plague her once again.

"He has poked his nose into my business more often than I care to admit," Morgan spat as the name hovered in the middle of the room. "He seemed to appear out of nowhere – a trivial annoyance, really – but just at the time when I was about to achieve everything that I had ever worked for. And then," she hissed, "with the aid of the Elementals, he helped to snatch it all away!"

"Speaking of the Elementals...," Eagler inquired.

"Do not concern yourself with them," Morgan said as she continued to glare at the burning letters. "They will be dealt with soon enough!"

"And the demon?" Eagler continued. "Have you given any thought to the Hedley boy?"

"Oh yes!" Morgan said as she began to brush the name of Ian Rimmel out of the air as though she had written them on a chalkboard. "I have something special..."

She stopped mid-sentence and stared curiously at the remaining letters that floated before her. She had swiped her hand across the name and several of the letters had disappeared, but not all of them; and mumbling to herself, she re-wrote the missing portions of letters and made the name whole again. Using her index finger, she began moving the letters around as if she were working on a jigsaw puzzle. Letters were placed in one position and then moved to another as she rearranged the name into several different words.

"Mistress," Sims asked as he looked on with concern, "is everything all right?"

Morgan moved the letters back and forth furiously; and as she did so, her skin grew pale. When she had finished, she looked at the phrase floating before her. Fear gripped her heart as she took a step back from the words of fire that levitated just inches from her face. Her fear was short-lived, however; quickly replaced with a fury that burned as hot as the sun.

Her screams of rage rang out so loudly that the cicada song was silenced. The insects, who moments before were calling out in a desperate search for a mate, would call out no more that night.

3. An Anagram all Along

Ian opened his eyes and looked around the room; surprised to feel cool, clean sheets against his skin. He climbed out of the bed shakily and observed his clothing, all of which had been cleaned and neatly folded, on a nightstand beside him. He dressed as quickly as he could and left the room on wobbly legs. Voices from down the hall guided him through the familiar house, as he made his way from the guest room to the home's modest dining room. As he entered the room, all eyes turned his way; some filled with relief while others were wide with shock.

"Good morning," Ian said weakly as he walked over to the dining room table and took a seat beside Tanna. "At least I assume it's morning, anyway."

"Close enough," Tanna said as she gave her guest a quick once over. "How are you feeling? Well enough to eat something, I hope..."

"Something to eat would be nice," Ian said gladly. "And coffee. Lots and lots of coffee!"

"Coming right up," Tanna said as she got up from the table. As she left for the kitchen she bent over and gave her old friend a kiss on the top of his head. "Welcome back!"

Ian chuckled softly and then turned his attention to the girls. They were all relieved to see him in better spirits, but he could see that they had questions. Questions that, as he stole a peek at the two newcomers at the table, he was not quite sure he could answer just yet.

"Hello ladies," he said with an all-knowing grin. "Let me guess; you all have used my current situation to your advantage and canceled your training for the day. Most likely due to your overwhelming concern for my general health and well-being."

"You know it!" Zoe said happily. "Never look a gift horse in the mouth! I mean…uh," she said blushing furiously, "what I meant was…"

"It's quite all right!" Ian said laughing. "And for the record, I am feeling much better today." Ian glanced over at the Sidhe who were also seated at the table, but for now had remained silent. He could tell from the way that they were staring at him that they were just as surprised as he was at seeing one another.

"Hello friends," he said amiably. "I am Ian Rimmel. I don't believe that I have had the pleasure…"

"I...I am Averyil; daughter of Eroquinn and Araniel. It is an honor to meet you, sir."

Ian nodded his head graciously as he glanced at Annalise and Zoe. "I thought I saw a resemblance. The honor, dear one, is mine. And you," he said as he faced Elwyn, "might you be Blair's brother, and thusly one of the heirs to the throne of Gorias?"

Elwyn stood up from the table as he continued staring at Ian. "What is this?" he demanded as he looked around the room. "Is this some sort of trick?!"

"It's no trick," Tanna said as she returned to the dining room with Ian's coffee. "I thought about explaining all of this to you earlier, but in the end, I believed it would be best if Ian told you everything himself."

"But," Elwyn exclaimed as he pointed at Ian, "this man is supposed to be dead!"

"Dead?" Ian said curiously. "Well, that certainly explains a lot."

"Please forgive me," Averyil said as she coaxed Elwyn back into his seat, "but I am not quite sure that I understand what, exactly, is happening. Are you...are you not...Merlin?"

"Yes," Ian said before taking a sip of his coffee, "and no. However, if you are about to tell me what I *think* you are about to tell me, then I suppose that, as of now, I am."

"Now you're confusing *me!*" Angelica groaned.

"My apologies, child." Ian grinned. He looked over at Averyil, serious once more. "Tell me of *your* Merlin's demise. I would like to know everything that has occurred since the Elementals returned here from Avalon.

Averyil glanced at Elwyn before beginning her tale. She told them all of King Korren's death, and how Lathos used the incident to enact martial law; literally crowning himself as the one true ruler of the Sidhe. Merlin had grown suspicious of Lathos' intentions shortly after he had left to supposedly destroy the Shadow King's mound. Instead, he had returned with an alleged treaty of peace with the Trolls. The only ones brought to heel that day were the Spriggan. Not one survived the massacre.

Merlin had begun to gather up those whom he believed were still loyal to the ideals brought forth by Alron. With the help of Gailon and Averyil, he formed an underground faction whose goal was to suppress the power and control that Lathos was attempting to amass. The wizard began visiting Elwyn, much to the chagrin of his older brother; and when she refused to have the visits stopped, Lathos had Nionia imprisoned as well.

Merlin had long believed that Lathos may have been the true Shadow King, and now that his accomplice had been drawn out, Merlin confronted the King of Gorias. Lathos immediately branded the wizard an enemy of the state and ordered him jailed, but the mage escaped. He stole a horse and fled the castle; followed closely by three of the king's most elite Riders. Eventually, Merlin had been deceived by Lathos' co-conspirator, who later returned to Gorias and announced the death of the once mighty wizard.

Upon hearing the news, Gailon and Averyil made their way to Gorias and broke Elwyn out of prison. Merlin had instructed them that if anything were to ever happen to him, Elwyn would be able to get them to the one person who could help them. However, during the prison break, they were set upon by a squad of troll soldiers. The battle was fierce and hard fought, with several of the trolls losing their lives; and even though Averyil and Elwyn were able to escape, Gailon was captured. The pair had to leave Gorias without ever learning his fate.

Before Averyil could go on any further, Blair had shifted into her Sidhe form. Her hair burned so brightly that the heat from it could be felt from across the entire room. Her eyes bore into her brother who was seated across from her. The force of her gaze was so intense that he unconsciously backed away from it.

"You allowed Lathos to lock up our mother?!" she growled.

"I allowed nothing!" Elwyn said in his own defense. "I,too, was a prisoner in the very same dungeon, if you recall!"

"Yeah, but you're *here* now!' Blair said angrily.

"I remember King Korren," Angelica said as she tried to defuse the budding argument. "We met him the day we left Avalon. How did he die?"

"He was found on his beloved archery range," Elwyn answered in an attempt to avoid his sister's scrutiny. "Someone had lashed him to a target before putting over fifty arrows into him!"

"Dear Gods," Ian said softly, "this has gotten out of hand."

"There is just one thing that I wish to know," Tanna said, her tone gruff. Everyone in the room turned in her direction, all but Ian. He kept his head down; as if he already knew what she was going to ask. "*Who* is this co-

conspirator? Who has Lathos enlisted to help him with all of this?"

"A vile witch," Averyil began. "Her name is..."

"...Morgan le Fay!" Tanna spat.

"Yes," Averyil stammered, "but how did *you* know?"

"I didn't," Tanna answered angrily as she glared at Ian, "but *you* did, didn't you?! You knew all along!"

"Merlin had his suspicions," Ian responded weakly. "He wished to see if he was correct. I merely assisted..."

"You knowingly exposed these girls to that...that *creature*! You sent them to Avalon, knowing that the prophecy had not yet begun, in the hopes of drawing her out. You used the Elementals as *bait*!" Tanna's anger was so great that she was visibly trembling.

"Lathos and Morgan are working together," Blair said, "and you *knew* all about it?!"

"You told us that the prophecy had begun," Zoe said angrily as she rose from her chair. "You lied to us!"

"You bewitched our parents," Eryn said as her temper began to flare, "and sent *us* on a wild goose chase!"

"Now listen," Ian said soothingly, "I can see that you all are upset, but if you just let me explain then everything will be clear to you. I promise!"

"You can begin by telling Averyil and I *who* or *what* you are!" Elwyn demanded. "No more riddles!"

"No more riddles," Ian agreed, "but perhaps a puzzle. An anagram."

"An anagram?" Averyil said curiously.

"Yes," Ian said quickly, "a phrase that, when the letters are rearranged, make an entirely *new* phrase. For instance, I have said that I am Merlin. Well, if you rearrange the letters in the phrase 'I am Merlin' you get..."

"Ian Rimmel!" Averyil answered.

"Exactly."

"That still does not explain how you came to be in two places at once," Elwyn barked.

"Some time ago, Merlin realized that something strange was going on in Avalon," Ian said. "He could not put his finger on it, but he knew that the focal point dwelt within the tribe of Gorias. Merlin was still overseeing the Elementals training, but he knew that he could not do that *and* conduct his investigation into Lathos' doings at the same time. So, as he had once before, he took on the guise of Ian Rimmel; only this time he needed to be in two places at once!"

"So he used a spell that split himself into two different people...," Zoe said.

"Precisely," Ian said as he looked around the room. "By splitting himself he could stay in Avalon while I came here to keep an eye on each of you. There were risks, but they were worth it."

"What sort of risks?" Annalise asked.

"While we remained two separate entities," Ian explained, "our powers – our magic – would grow weaker. To alleviate this problem, I would simply return to Avalon periodically. Once there, we would become one being again; in this way, we could replenish our magic. After a week or two, we would separate again and I would return here."

"That would explain why no one can recall seeing Merlin using any magic for some time," Averyil stated.

"Yes," Ian said. "It has been some time since I last traveled to Avalon; we grew weaker the longer we were apart."

"Well," Elwyn said, "it would seem that the two of you used magic to get us into this situation; why do you not use magic to get us out of it? Take this witch, this Morgan le Fay, down once and for all!"

"That," Ian said pensively, "could be a bit of a problem. You see, my powers are no more. I can no longer wield magic."

"Wait...what?!" Eryn exclaimed.

"My recent episodes of illness. My bouts of extreme fatigue and dizziness. It all falls into place now that I know the Merlin half of me is dead. I have lost the ability to use my magic."

"Leaving these girls at the mercy of a monster!" Tanna said, clearly enraged.

"Did he – *we* – put you all at risk?" Ian said defensively. "Yes, perhaps we did. Should I have stepped in and tried to prevent Merlin from going through with his plan when I learned of what his intentions were? Probably so, but what was done, I'm sure, was done for the greater good of all involved; at least," he said as his voice trailed off, "I thought so at the time."

"If that was an attempt at trying to sound remorseful ," Tanna said bitterly, "you had better try again!"

"So there is no way for you to regain your powers?" Averyil asked.

"There is *one* way...," Ian said.

"The Book of E'lythmarium," Annalise chimed in.

"Yes," he answered. "If I were to retrieve the Book of E'lythmarium from its hiding place, I could begin the process that would allow me to regain all of my powers — and then some."

"Well then," Elwyn said, "why do we not go and retrieve this book so we can restore your powers to you?"

"That," Ian said, "brings us to another problem."

*　　*　　*

"She's dead, isn't she?" Erik asked fearfully as he took a step back. His eyes grew wide as he looked at all of the damage he had caused. "I...I didn't mean to do it — I swear!"

Dan walked over and stood beside the panic-stricken teen as he looked down at the mess that laid at their feet. "It wasn't your fault," the foreman said hoping to calm the boy down. "But I don't think that we will be able to keep this a secret; do you, Erik?"

"I guess not," Erik said with a shrug of his shoulders. "Man – my dad is gonna be ticked!"

Dan leaned over and took a closer look at the irrigation unit. The device was now covered in hydraulic fluid; the sticky red substance dripped off the sides of the machine and formed a puddle underneath it. "He might get a little upset," Dan said as he tapped the unit with a screwdriver, "but that's just the cost of doin' business. The real culprit is this old switch gauge."

"You really think so?" Erik asked as he bent over to take a look. He was relieved to know that he had not screwed something else up around the orchard during his first day of 'on the job training.' "I mean, there's no doubt in your mind that this switch-a-ma-gig is broken?"

"Relax," Dan said with a smile. "I've had problems with it before. The diaphragm's bad; I'm sure of it!"

"The diaphragm?" Erik asked curiously. "What does that do?"

"Well," Dan explained, "the switch gauge helps monitor the irrigation unit's engine, air, and hydraulic pressure. The diaphragm, which is inside the gauge, helps protect the unit from blowing a gasket, so to speak. The diaphragm in this particular gauge is screwed up, so we weren't getting an accurate reading on the hydraulic pressure – so when you turned it on…"

Erik's expression said it all; his eyes were glassy and his mouth hung open limply.

"You could care less about any of this; am I right?" Dan asked, laughing.

"Was I that obvious?" Erik answered with a smile. "So, I didn't break the unit?"

"Nope," Dan replied as he clapped the boy on the back, "not this time anyway!"

Erik looked at the foreman and frowned; the light-hearted moment shortlived. He turned and began walking away.

"Hey," Dan called, "where do you think you're goin'?"

"Who am I kidding?" Erik asked looking back at Dan. "This isn't me! I'm not a farmer. It would take me years to learn all of this stuff!"

"Which is why your old man wanted you to start spending more time with me. You're not goin' to get any of this overnight, believe me!"

"But I'm not like him," Erik said, speaking about his father. "I don't want to be like him...a farmer, I mean."

Dan gave the boy a knowing look. "I know *exactly* what you mean. Believe me when I tell you that you will *never* be like your father!"

"You really think so?" Erik asked.

"I know so," Dan said. "Your dad wasn't always like he is now. Once upon a time, he was a lot like you. But things change – people change. Your dad always had big dreams for this place, and he was determined to make them a reality. No matter what.

"He kicked, bit, punched, and clawed his way to the head of the class. He's a phenomenal business man and one heck of a farmer." Dan paused for a moment before continuing. "You don't get to the top of your game like he did without making some enemies."

"You don't make very many friends, either." Erik said, his tone surly.

"No," Dan agreed. "No, you don't." He placed his hand on Erik's shoulder and gave it a shake. "What do you say we get this unit fixed? Okay?"

"Okay," Erik said, grinning slightly.

Dan smiled at the boy as he reached into his back pocket and withdrew a two-way radio. The tiny device squeaked when he pressed the button on the side. "Mike, it's Dan. You on here?"

Several seconds of silence ticked by before he got a response. "Yeah," Mike answered, "I'm here. Whatcha got, Dan?"

"I'm up on the northeast corner with Erik and we've got a busted irrigation unit…"

"Switch gauge finally blew, huh?" Mike said over the radio. "I didn't think that it would hold out for much longer."

"Well, she finally bit the dust. Do you think you can come here and take a look at it?"

"Sure thing," Mike answered. "I'm just finishing up with the broken split rails here by the lake – I can be there in about twenty minutes."

"Sounds good," Dan said. "I'll stick around and wait for you to show up." The radio squeaked once more as they cleared the channel.

"So now we wait," Erik said glumly.

"Oh, I don't think that we both need to stay here and wait for Mike," Dan said. "Besides, I'm pretty sure there is someplace else you'd rather be right now. Am I right?"

Erik's cheeks reddened as a smile crept onto his face. "Seriously – are you for real?"

"I won't tell your dad if you won't!" Dan said with a wink.

"Yes!" Erik yelled as he turned on his heels and hurried off.

The creature watched them from within the cherry trees; far enough away and down wind so the boy would not catch its scent. Even though his kind was undetectable to the demon, the shadowy figure did not want to take any chances. It had ben sent here to observe its target. *Watch him,* it thought to itself, *track him, observe his movements; but do not lure him – no, not yet.*

It watched in silence as the boy spoke to the older human. For a moment, it took its eyes off of the boy and gazed longingly at the man who stood nearby. Its stomach growled violently as it took a step toward the two, but the creature concealed itself deeper in the shadows of the trees and fought off its pangs of hunger.

So long, it sighed miserably, *so long since the last feeding. The male would be easy prey, but the boy – no. It is not time. Not quite time...*

The creature watched as the man took something from his pocket and began speaking into it. Only bits and pieces of his conversation made its way to the area where the thing of myth concealed itself, but it heard one thing that was said as clearly as if it had been standing beside the human male. Its mouth began to salivate as it crept deeper into the darkness provided by the trees. It took one last look at the boy, and then it turned and ran off. Away it went, towards the lake – for now, it could feed.

Mike had finished putting the last split rail into place, and now the fence was fixed. He began putting his tools into the back of his truck and was preparing to go and meet Dan when he heard a noise. Turning toward the lake, he glanced about; and when he located the source of the strange sound he could not believe his eyes.

Standing a short distance from the lake was a beautiful black horse. Its silky mane hung low from its head, and the wind-blown hair danced across the animal's well-muscled neck and withers. The horse dipped its head and then raised it up again, looking over at Mike expectantly. Its eyes, as black as onyx, locked onto Mike's and seemed to beckon him.

Entranced, Mike walked slowly over to the animal. He moved carefully, so as to not scare it off. As he grew closer, the horse whinnied, and Mike put his hands up in an effort to calm the horse. "It's okay, beautiful! I'm not going to hurt you. No, old Mike is your friend!"

The horse quieted down but did not take its eyes off of the man approaching it. As Mike drew nearer, he was swept away by the horse's beauty. He could see that the animal had been well cared for. From its appearance, it could very well have been a show horse. He did notice, however, that there were some weeds in its mane; and when he reached out to remove them he realized that they were wet.

Mike felt drawn to look into the animal's eyes and when he did it felt as though the horse was speaking to him. There was a hint of, what Mike believed to be, jasmine in the air; and an overwhelming impulse to climb up onto the majestic beast took him by storm. The horse pawed the ground with its hooves, as though it longed for a run. Unable to control the urge any longer, Mike climbed up onto its back. He wrapped his fingers within the thick silky mane and clamped his legs tightly against either side of the muscular animal. Without any prompting, as if it were acting on pure instinct, the horse took off at a full gallop.

An intense feeling of euphoria grabbed hold of Mike as the horse ran full tilt toward the lake. As they grew closer to the water's edge, Mike pulled the animal's mane in an attempt to turn it away from the body of water that they were fast approaching. Instead of turning, however, the horse picked up its pace, hurtling toward the lake at break-neck speed.

Mike increased his efforts, but nothing that he did caused the beast to stop. He tried to dismount, but his legs felt as if they had been glued into place with some strangely unyielding adhesive. He dug his fingers deeper into the horse's mane and pulled back with all of his might. The animal's head reared back, but it continued on its deadly course. Mike caught a glimpse of its face in that instant and when he did, he screamed. Gone were the dark black beautiful eyes. Now, they were a bright red; like two embers in a smelting furnace. Its teeth were not the teeth of a horse, but more like the fangs of an alligator – large, white, and sharp.

The creature ran into the lake, its hooves slapping the surface of the water. Unbelievably, it did not fall in but continued out into the middle of the lake. When it reached the center, it rose onto its hind legs and let loose with a horrendous screech. Mike screamed out for help one last time before the animal leaped up into the air; and then, it came crashing down into the water, retreating with its prize to the bottom of the lake.

With his dying breath, Mike watched as the surface of the lake grew further and further away. Undeterred, and now finally able to feed, the creature carried him down to the dark murky depths below. Feeling its prey go slack, it released its hold on the human; and as they drifted down into the darkness the creature began tearing Mike's flesh apart.

4. Of Books and Beasts

There were moments, times such as this, where Eagler could feel the witch's hold on him weaken. During these – gaps – he would quietly try to slip away from her control. He was not alone. As he was pulling up to the cabin with something for Morgan to eat, he noticed Sims standing on the front porch. It was evident from the expression on his friend's face that he was experiencing the same sensation – the witch's focus was elsewhere. Perhaps now, if they worked together, they could be free.

Neither one of the two men particularly liked the things that she made them do. The thoughts that she put into their heads went against everything that they knew, trusted, and believed in. One day soon, if they were lucky, she would become so enthralled with her search for the mysterious Ian Rimmel that her concentration on the two of *them* would wane. Then, maybe then, they would have a possibility of escape, but it would not be today. Once again, she felt them trying to pull away. Once again, she tightened her grip on them.

Eagler pulled the car up to the stairs that led up to the front porch and put the vehicle into park. He climbed out of the car, went around to the passenger side, and retrieved the bag of food from the front seat.

"Any news...?" Sims asked as his partner climbed up the stairs.

"Nothing," Eagler replied. "All of the hotels, motels, B&B's and hospitals have been checked. Patrol's come up empty."

"She's not going to like that," Sims said as he glanced at Eagler from the corner of his eye.

"You don't think I already know that!" Eagler grumbled. "Just keep an eye on the road," he growled as he went inside the cabin.

He made his way toward the rear of the cottage where he found Morgan, standing in front of a large set of sliding glass doors staring out at the lake. Eagler placed the food down onto the dining room table and stood by silently, waiting to be acknowledged. He could feel the tension coming off of her in waves. Since she discovered this Ian Rimmel's true identity, Morgan had been in a state of anxiety the likes of which he had never witnessed before.

Her initial outburst at discovering the truth was one of anger – the intensity of it so great that she nearly destroyed the cabin. None of the furniture in the front two rooms had been left intact. A large, gaping hole in the floor greeted those who came through the front door; Eagler had to jump over the eight-foot gap in order to get to the back of the house. There were savage-looking gashes in the walls, vicious marks that had been made as furniture – some as heavy as a hundred pounds – had crashed into them as they flew about the room. She had unleashed the full fury of her magic; and when she was spent she fell to the floor in a heap. She had stayed that way until the next morning when she had sent Eagler out for news of her enemy's whereabouts.

"Please tell me," she said quietly as she continued to stare out at the lake, "that you have news of Merlin."

"I'm sorry," Eagler apologized. He held his head up high, his shoulders back. After all, he had done nothing wrong.

"You are *sorry...?*" Morgan hissed as she turned to face him.

"The patrol units have been looking everywhere," he tried to explain. "The hotels, the inns, even the hospitals – the man's a ghost!"

"He is not a *man*, you idiot!" Morgan yelled as she swept the bag of food from the table, sending it across the room where it splattered against the wall. "He is the most powerful wizard your world has ever seen!" She stormed around the table and stood directly in front of him. He thought it wise not to make eye contact.

"Why," she snarled, "do I continue to put my faith in you useless mortals?!"

"With the girls here," Eagler countered, "it's highly doubtful that he would leave town. Where would he possibly go?"

"How am I supposed to know that?" Morgan shouted. "This is *your* city! Why do you need my assistance for a relatively simple..."

"Sorry to interrupt," Sims said as he poked his head through the front door. "We just got a call. Something's going on at the Hedley place. Something big!"

"The Hedley home!" Morgan said excitedly. Perhaps her spy had discovered something. "There is your answer, Captain! Proceed to the Hedley farm. I believe it is *there* that you will find the answers that I seek!"

* * *

"So," Erik asked as he locked eyes with Ian, "what are the chances of Morgan being here in Traverse City right now?"

"I would think that the chances are quite high," Ian said matter-of-factly. He was somewhat surprised at how calm Erik had remained as he was brought up to speed by Ian and the others. *You have definitely come a long way,* he thought to himself. "If I were her, I would make my way here as quickly as possible."

"Why is that?" Eryn asked, afraid that she already knew the answer.

"Because with Merlin dead," Erik replied, "the only things powerful enough to stand in her way are us." He continued to stare at Ian. "She's coming for us, isn't she?"

"I'm afraid so, young Master Hedley."

"Let her come," Annalise said bitterly. "We can take care of ourselves!"

"Yes," Ian said, "but it will not just be *you* that she will come after. She'll come for everything that you hold dear first – your friends, your family – no one will be safe!"

"And what of you, Wizard?" Averyil asked. "Once she learns of *your* existence your life too will be forfeit."

"That is true," Ian agreed. "Without my powers, she would crush me like an insect. But for now, I am counting on the fact that she is unaware of my existence; or at the very least, my current location and condition."

"Then we need to get to the Book of E'lythmarium," Erik said eagerly, "and restore your magic before she can find you!"

"Believe me, Erik, the Book of E'lythmarium is closer than you think." Ian said.

"So with this book," Elwyn said as he approached Ian. A sharp glance from Erik stopped the prince in his tracks. "So with this book," Elwyn said as he cleared his throat, "you will not only retrieve your own powers but the magical abilities of every great wizard and witch that ever came before you?"

"That's correct," Ian said with a nod of his head. "Whosoever possesses the Book of E'lythmarium, *and* can unlock its secrets, would become the most powerful witch or warlock of all time. They could rule this universe, and others, if they so chose!"

"So it is imperative that Morgan does not get her hands on it," Averyil said.

"I can only imagine the countless number of worlds that she would destroy if she were to have access to power such as that," Ian said gravely.

"But we can trust *you* with this power," Elwyn said sarcastically. "Is that what you are saying, wizard?"

"Hello pot," Erik said under his breath as he moved away from Elwyn and Ian, "my name's kettle…"

"I am well aware that none of you trust me," Elwyn said as he looked around the room, "and I accept the fact that I have my work cut out for me if I am to regain your respect; but we are talking about giving one man the powers of the Gods! How can we be sure that he is able to take on such a responsibility?"

"The mere fact that I have had access to the Book of E'lythmarium all of this time and have never been tempted to take its power as my own should be answer enough," Ian said calmly.

"So you say," Elwyn went on, "but where *is* this precious book? How do we know that you actually have access to it?"

"It's been here with us this entire time," Ian said, "and I haven't bothered to repossess it."

"You...you hid the book here at my house?" Tanna asked.

"No," Ian answered. "It was not hidden in your house."

"Then where is it?" Angelica asked.

"The one place that Morgan wouldn't dare go to recover it," Ian said as he walked over to Erik and Zoe, "even *if* she knew of its location."

"Really Ian, enough with the games," Zoe said, exasperated. "Where is it?!"

"I thought by now that the answer would have been obvious," Ian said as he stared at Erik and tapped him on the forehead. "It's all right up here!"

"What?" Tanna exclaimed.

"I...I don't understand," Erik stammered. "You put the Book of E'lythmarium inside my *head*?!"

"Think about it dear boy," Ian said. "Why do you think I took you on as my apprentice? How do you think a mortal – born and raised in the world of Man – could obtain the magical ability that you have displayed? It is impossible, unless...!"

"Erik has *no* magic ability?" Blair asked, shocked.

"Only that which has sprung forth from the book," Ian replied. "I had to teach him how to wield his newfound abilities safely; otherwise, the lad could have done some serious damage."

"Right now," Tanna hissed, "I am at a loss as to which is the cruelest creature to ever live – Morgan le Fay or you, Ian!"

"I did not *want* to do it, Tanna!" Ian tried to explain. "But the Book is safest within Erik; don't you see that?"

"No," Erik said confused, "I don't see at all. Try explaining it to me.."

"You survived the bite of the Hellhound, boy." Ian said, turning to him. "There are beings of great power – Morgan being one of them – that are absolutely terrified of you, and what you have become. Even if she became aware of the Book of E'lythmarium's whereabouts she wouldn't dare attempt to go after it. It might sound crass, but you were – and are – the most secure repository the Book of E'lythmarium has ever been placed in!"

"That's twisted, Ian." Zoe said angrily. "Even for you!"

"Okay everybody," Erik said loudly, "that's enough!" He glared icily at Ian. "Now that we know where the Book is, you can have it back. I don't want it!"

"Yes!" Elwyn said excitedly. "You can recover your powers; and together, we can put a stop to this witch, Morgan le Fay, and my duplicitous elder brother and his illicit scheme!"

"I told you before," Ian went on, "it's not as simple as that."

The guilt in Ian's voice filled Erik with dread. "Why?" he asked. "Why isn't it simple?"

"You might recall," Ian said sadly, "that there's a reason why no one is allowed to survive after being bitten by a Hellhound. They eventually lose control to the beast within. They can hold on for a matter of hours – sometimes even a few days – but the demon always wins; and once it does, there is no turning back."

"But Erik has maintained control for more than a year," Zoe said. "He's not a monster!"

"He's not a monster," Ian said, "because the Book of E'lythmarium gives him the ability to keep the beast reigned in. Remove the book, and he..."

"Becomes a demon," Erik said softly; his eyes blank and glassy as he stared off into the distance.

Tanna walked over to Ian and placed a hand upon his shoulder. Her earlier feelings of anger and betrayal fading; she was now filled with a sense of understanding and rekindled admiration. "You did not place the Book of E'lythmarium within Erik to keep *it* safe, did you? You placed it there to keep the demon at bay. You never intended to remove it at all."

"No," Ian said. "I relinquished the Book to save the boy; and now...and now it seems that all of that was for naught."

"So we have two options," Elwyn said as he stared at Erik, "we remove the Book and use its power to defeat Morgan le Fay – sacrificing the boy in the process..."

"Or," Zoe said defensively, "we leave the book where it is and find some other way to beat Morgan!"

"I must admit," Ian said shakily, his cavalier attitude gone, "that I am at a loss as to what to do." He looked at Erik with doleful eyes. "I am so sorry, my boy. I've bloody well bodged this all up, haven't I? If I had been able to foresee *any* of this..."

Erik walked over to Ian and hugged him tightly. "You don't have to apologize to me," he said smiling warmly as he came to realize what his mentor had sacrificed in order to save his life. "I can see now that you only did what you thought was right. I want you to know that I..."

Erik was interrupted by his cell phone ringing. He reached into his pocket, took out the phone and looked at the display; muttering under his breath when he saw the name on the screen. He tapped the glass face firmly before putting the phone to his ear.

"Yeah, Dad?" he said exasperated. Erik was quiet for a moment before he said, "I'm with Zoe. We're just hanging out..."

The others stood quietly by as Erik's forehead grew furrowed. He took the phone away from his ear and stared at it incredulously before he spoke again. "Slow down a second! I...I don't know what you're talking about!"

Erik glanced at Ian and the others; shrugging his shoulders in confusion as his father continued yelling on the other end. "I never...," Erik tried to say, "I never showed...I don't *know*!" He nodded his head angrily as he continued to speak, "We're not far; we can be there in a few minutes. Yes...yes...OKAY!" Erik hit the screen with his finger and slammed the phone back into his pocket.

"What was that?" Zoe asked anxiously.

"Something's going on at the orchard," Erik said hotly, "my dad wants me there ASAP!" He looked at Zoe hopefully. "Do you mind coming with me?"

"Of course not," she said.

"Your father sounded quite agitated," Ian said. "Is everything all right?"

"I'm not sure," Erik answered. "All he would say was that the place was swarming with police and that he needed me there!"

"This cannot be good," Tanna said as she glanced at Ian. "Do you think that Morgan has regained control of Chief Whipple?"

"I know that she hasn't," Ian said cryptically. "But," he said to Erik and Zoe, "you two need to remain vigilant. I have a bad feeling about this – please, be careful!"

"You don't have to tell us twice!" Zoe said nervously.

*　　*　　*

Erik and Zoe exited the portal from the far side of the house; far enough away from curious eyes. They made their way around to the front of the house and then took a well-worn path that Erik knew would get them to the lake much faster than if they had used one of the small golf carts that his father left around for quick jaunts around the property.

As they made their way toward the lake, Zoe gasped when she saw the large number of police officers milling about. Some were digging around in the brush alongside of a split rail fence, some were taking pictures of a pickup truck and the lake itself; while others still were standing about, talking amongst themselves. Erik located his father, he was speaking with Dan and two other officers; and taking Zoe by the hand, led her in that direction.

"Dad, Dan...," Erik said as they approached the four men, "...what's going on? Why are the police here?"

Erik took notice of the two police officers who had been speaking with his father. They were both very imposing individuals; their faces masks of bored indifference – that is until they saw the two teens walking over to them. Their eyes were hidden behind mirrored sunglasses, even though the late afternoon sky was overcast; and while one of the men threw off an air of cautious discernment, the other one grinned a freakish toothy grin. His demeanor caused the hairs on the back of Erik's neck to stiffen. Erik could not see the man's eyes because of the reflective surface of the lenses in his glasses, but he could sense the officer's excited anticipation; as though he were a ravenous lion about to make a kill. Acting purely on instinct, Erik placed himself purposefully between this particular officer and Zoe.

"Well, well, well...," Sims said, still grinning insidiously, "look at what the cat dragged in!"

"Captain Sims, Captain Eagler...," Junior said nervously as he walked over and stood beside Zoe and his son, "this is my boy, Erik; and his girlfriend, Zoe..."

"Beckford," Eagler said as he appraised the two teenagers carefully, "yes; we know who you are."

"I'm sorry, but do I know you?" Zoe asked suspiciously.

"Probably not," Sims said quickly. "He must have heard your name somewhere around town; isn't that right, Captain Eagler!"

"Yeah," Eagler growled, upset at his gaff. "That's it, exactly."

"So what's going on?" Erik asked as he searched the men's faces for answers.

"Mike has gone missing," Junior said, "and the police suspect foul play. We can't find him anywhere. It's as if he just fell off the face of the Earth!"

"Mike?" Erik said confused. "We were just talking to him this morning."

"We?" Eagler asked. "Who's 'we'?"

"That would be me," Dan answered. "I was with Erik this morning when we spoke to Mike on the two-way."

"I was talking to the boy!" Eagler said loudly. He took a moment to compose himself before he continued; acknowledging the fact that everyone was staring at him. "Perhaps Captain Sims has some questions."

Sims nodded his head and stepped forward. "One might say that there have been some strange goings-on around your orchard. Wouldn't you agree, Mr. Hedley?"

"What kind of strange goings-on?" Junior asked, gruffly.

"C'mon now," Sims said smiling, " surely you've heard the stories. Weird sounds, strange lights in the middle of the night; and let's not forget the 'Wicked winged Demon of Hedley Farm'!"

"Those are just stories!" Junior protested as he cut his eyes angrily at Dan. "Stupid myths cooked up by people with too much time on their hands!"

"Probably so," Sims said with a bored tone to his voice. He began to turn away, but stopped and glanced at Erik. "So what do *you* think happened to your farm hand? Kind of odd, him just disappearing like that."

"I...I don't know what happened to him," Erik said nervously. "All I know is that he was talking with me and Dan on the two-way before I left to see Zoe."

"That's right," Dan said nodding his head. "It's just like Mr. Hedley said; it's like Mike vanished without a trace."

"Oh, I wouldn't say that," Sims sneered. He walked over to a spot near the edge of the lake that had been roped off. He stopped next to the police tape and stared down at the ground. "No one just vanishes. There's always a little something that we all leave behind."

The officer stooped down and looked out at the lake. "Tell me, Erik. Have you ever seen viscera?"

"Excuse me?" Erik said, confused.

"Viscera," Sims repeated. "C'mon big guy, you know what I'm talking about. Entrails...offal...bowels – you know – guts! We found some here, you know."

"I...I don't know what you mean...," Erik stammered, taken aback.

"Sure you do," Sims teased the wicked smile back on his face. "If there is anyone here that would know what it is that I'm talking about it would be you!"

"My son just said that he has no idea what you are talking about!" Junior said angrily. "Are you calling him a liar?"

"Of course not," Sims said, "perish the thought." He rubbed his hand in the grass that was inside the taped off area, and then standing up, walked over to Erik. "I'm just proceeding with a line of questioning."

He stood in front of Erik for a moment, saying nothing, before he stuck his hand in the boy's face. "You smell that?"

"N...no," Erik lied, "what is it?" He did his best not to react to the pungent, ruddy odor that hit his sense of smell like a freight train – firing off the synapses of his brain like a fireworks display on the fourth of July. The coppery smell of human blood seized hold of the monster within him, and it took all of his resolve to keep it in check.

"You really don't know?" Sims eyed the boy warily, waiting for the reaction that he knew was coming; but Junior put an end to his little game.

"I don't know what you are trying to pull off here, Captain Sims; but whatever it is, it ends now!"

"You're right, Mr. Hedley." Sims said as he continued to stare at Erik. He wiped his hand on his pant leg before turning to face the irate father. "Sometimes I get a bit carried away."

"Well," Junior fumed, "we'll see if Chief Whipple can help you with that little character flaw when I call him to discuss your behavior!"

"There's no reason for everyone to get all worked up," Eagler said, trying to smooth things over. "Perhaps its time we start wrapping things up here."

"I think that is a good idea," Junior agreed. "You and your men need to leave and get down to business. I have a man missing and I want him found!"

"We'll do our best, sir." Eagler said through gritted teeth.

"Ms. Beckford," Sims said to Zoe with an amiable smile, "we're heading back into town. Would you care for a lift?"

"Yes," Eagler said as he placed a hand on the girl's shoulder and turned her toward the car. "That's an excellent idea. Right this way, young lady. Besides, I believe there is another matter that you can help us with…"

"Excuse me," Junior said, stopping the men in their tracks, "but Zoe is our guest this evening. She's having dinner with us and staying for a movie. I'll make sure that she gets home, afterward."

Eagler glared at Junior for what seemed an eternity before looking down at the obviously scared, and anxious girl at his side. "Is this true?"

"Y…yes," Zoe stammered, going along with Junior's fabrication. "Erik invited me over several days ago."

Sims approached the pair; his face cloaked in disbelief. "You're actually staying for dinner?" he asked Zoe skeptically. "After all of this nasty business? There's blood and gore all over the place!"

"I've got a strong stomach," Zoe answered.

Eagler sized Zoe up, examining her as though she were a lab specimen before he removed his hand from her shoulder and stepped away. "Very well." He glanced over at Sims. "Time for us to go."

The two police officers climbed into their vehicle and buckled themselves in. The engine roared to life and Eagler put the car into gear; hesitating a moment as he rolled down the driver's side window.

"We'll let you know if there are any further developments in our investigation, Mr. Hedley." he said gruffly as he stared at Junior. "And if we have any further questions..."

"You can address them with my attorney!" Junior barked.

Eagler nodded his head and rolled the window up again. Bits of sod shot from beneath the rear tires of the car as the wheels spun, gaining traction; and once upon the roadway, the car weaved around one of the mobile crime units and sped off down the lane.

Junior, Dan, Erik, and Zoe watched the officers drive off with a collective sigh of relief. As the vehicle rolled out of sight, Junior and Dan turned and made their way to Mike's pickup truck.

"Mr. Hedley," Zoe called out.

Junior turned and looked at Zoe and his son. "Yes?"

"Thank you," Zoe said gratefully. "I definitely did not feel comfortable around those two guys!"

"There was no way in the world that I was going to allow you to leave with those two, Zoe." Junior said as he walked over to her. He took a look at his son before giving his arm a squeeze. "You okay?"

"Yeah," Erik said with a slight nod of his head.

"Well," Junior continued as he turned back to Dan and the truck, "you better let your mom and Sandy know that we will be having a guest for dinner – that is if you don't mind staying, Zoe; *and* you get your parents permission."

"Yes sir," they both said as Junior and Dan began giving the truck a once over. Zoe looked at Erik, who was staring at his father in stunned silence before she gave his arm a tug.

"What's gotten into you?" she asked worriedly. "Are you still freaked out about those two cops?"

"No," Erik said. "I'm just trying to figure out who that guy is over there that looks like my dad!"

"Stop it," Zoe laughed. "I think it's cool that he stood up for you like that!"

"*And* you," Erik gushed. "I still can't get over how protective he seemed to be over you!"

"Don't look a gift horse in the mouth," Zoe said for the second time that day as Erik took her by the hand and they began to walk back toward the house.

"Yeah, I guess so, but we are gonna have to tell Ian and Tanna about all of this as soon as we can. Something isn't right, and he might just have some answers for us."

The two of them made their way back to the house, ignoring the police officers who were packing up all of their gear and equipment – ostensibly finished with their evidence collecting. One officer, however, seemed to take an unusual amount of interest in the boy and girl as they walked away. He watched them until they disappeared from sight, and then he turned and made his way toward the orchards; the grass tickling his bare feet and the collar of his uniform shirt soaked from the water that dripped from his jet black hair.

5. The Kelpie

Eagler sat at his desk, his hands clenched tightly into fists and his back ramrod straight, as he glared down at the photos scattered across its surface. The faces of the girls, Erik, and the woman he knew as Olivia Solorio stared back at him; each subject caught in a different pose that had been taken over a period of the last several days.

He had originally taken the pictures so as to familiarize himself with his quarry, but he had no idea when he was taking them that the answer to his initial riddle had been staring him right in the face all along. Eagler picked up a thumb tack from the corner of his desk and slowly pushed it through the face of one of the pictures of Angelica's grandmother, Olivia. The fierce intensity of his anger swelled as he stared at the woman's image. He found it hard to believe that he had not pieced it all together before now.

The knifelike stench of ozone forced its way through his mopish introspection, causing his nostrils to flare. He cocked an eye across the room at the portal that was opening up upon the far wall and scowled. *Looks like my leash is being pulled again,* he thought bitterly to himself.

He scooped up the pictures and slid them into a file folder before placing it into one of the drawers of his desk.

Pulling himself out of his chair, Eagler walked over to the rift and stepped inside. When he came out on the other end he observed Morgan le Fay standing at the edge of the lake. She was looking out at the landscape beyond the water's edge, and she was not alone. A man with thick black hair and dark features stood beside her. There was a malicious air about him, and Eagler could not help but notice that he was wearing a Traverse City Police uniform.

"Captain Eagler," Morgan chirped, "how nice of you to join us this morning!"

"Good morning, Mistress." Eagler said as he stared icily at the man beside her. "May I ask who this is, and where he got one of my departmental uniform's from?"

"Oh," she said as if she only just realized that she was not alone, "this is Malo. As for the uniform...you probably do not want to know how he gained possession of it."

Eagler stared at her for a moment, taking time to reign in his temper before answering. "So be it, my lady." He stood there, waiting, as Morgan and her guest continued to ignore him. "I may have some news in regard to Ian Rimmel," he said through gritted teeth.

"Now I *am* intrigued," Morgan said as she finally turned and faced the officer. "What, exactly, have you learned?"

Eagler took a deep breath. "I believe that he may be hiding out at the home of a Ms. Olivia Solorio. She is the grandmother…"

"Yes, yes, yes." Morgan interrupted. "She is the grandmother of the Earth-wielder."

"Yes," Eagler acknowledged sourly, "yes she is. I have not pieced together how she fits in with the sorcerer yet – unless she is aware of her granddaughter's secret."

"Aware of it?" Morgan spat. "You fool; she *shares* it! Olivia Solorio is a Sidhe!"

"What?!" Eagler asked, feeling gut-punched.

"Her given name is Tanna," the stranger beside Morgan said with a deep, gravelly voice. "She is of the tribe of Falias. She has been living as one of you for quite some time."

"And how would *you* know?" Eagler asked angrily; but the man paid no attention to him, choosing to go silent once more as he gazed out at the lake.

"You have just confirmed information that Malo brought to me late last evening, Captain Eagler." Morgan said with a smile. "It seems that he overheard a conversation between the Hedley boy and his girlfriend while he was out at the farm. From it, he deduced that Merlin is indeed hiding at the home of the Sidhe."

"He...he was at *my* crime scene?" Eagler bristled as he pointed his finger at Malo.

"Of course he was," Morgan replied. "I have spies everywhere."

"Well," Eagler asked as he bored holes through the stranger's back with his eyes, "do you plan on confronting the wizard?"

"No," she responded. "Since he has yet to make a move against me I must assume that he is unaware of my presence here. I would keep it that way – at least until I am ready to strike!"

Morgan walked over to him. "I want you to keep your eyes open. Even as we speak, Sims is already outside the house, watching, in an attempt to assess their next move. I do not wish for either of you to accost them without my permission. Is that understood?"

"Yes, Mistress."

"Excellent," Morgan said as she opened another portal and gestured toward it. "Off you go then, Captain. Back to work!"

Eagler bowed his head slightly and made his way to the portal's entrance. He took a moment before stepping into the rift and looked fixedly in Malo's direction. He could tell that the other man was intentionally ignoring him, but because he had no real idea about the relationship between Morgan and the stranger, he left them without saying another word.

Morgan watched as the portal closed behind the police officer, and then her eyes flashed over at the man who remained standing silently at the water's edge. She sauntered over until she was once again standing beside him; her mouth pinched into a devilishly playful smile.

"You are quiet, Malo." she mocked. "Even more so than usual."

"I speak when I have something to say," the man said, refusing to be baited. Drops of water fell from his hair as he looked out at the lake – and freedom.

"You were rather rude to Captain Eagler. You really should learn to play nicely with others."

"I do not play with my food," Malo growled.

"Now *that* is funny!" Morgan said, laughing.

"You humor easily," Malo said with a scowl.

"Maybe," Morgan said with a more serious tone, "I should send *you* into that house after Merlin. That would be humorous!"

"That," Malo said as his lip curled in disgust, "would be a fool's errand."

"I could *make* you, you know!" Morgan grinned cruelly.

"As long as you hold the bridle," Malo said as his face grew dark, "you can make me do anything that you desire!"

"Yes," Morgan said, "but I am merely having fun at your expense. I meant what I said earlier, I have no intention of divulging my presence to Merlin just yet. He is up to something; I can *feel* it!

"No. For now, I want you to maintain your vigil over the abomination – Erik Hedley. That is why you are here;

the demon cannot sense your presence. It is that reason, and that alone, which makes you my most perfect spy!"

"Do you believe that this boy has the Book of E'lythmarium?" Malo asked as he turned to her."

"No," Morgan answered, "but I am almost certain that he knows where it is hidden. The old goat most likely has the boy guarding it for him!"

"If the boy has any knowledge to the book's location," Malo said, "I will find out."

"I know that you will," Morgan grinned. "Remember; find me the Book and I will return the bridle to you!"

*   *   *

The entire household rose early that morning at Tanna's; and although the house remained quiet, there was tension in the air. Within an hour after the morning meal, the girls began to arrive. As they greeted one another, a portal opened up in the kitchen and Erik stepped out, acknowledging everyone with a nod of his head.

"Erik...," Tanna said with a note of disapproval in her voice.

"Sorry," Erik apologized, remembering his promise not to use portals inside her house. Tanna had a hard time getting the smell out of the place.

"So, Master Hedley," Ian inquired eagerly, "what have you...any news?"

Erik glanced over at Zoe before he recounted their ordeal at the orchard the previous evening. The expressions on his friends' faces were grave as he told his story, and when he came to the end Ian requested that he tell the tale one more time. The wizard insisted that Erik describe everything in detail that transpired at the lake. Erik did as he was asked, and when he finished with his account, Ian turned and began pacing the floor; a worried look furrowing his brow.

"What is it, Ian?" Tanna asked nervously. "Do you have any idea what is going on?"

"Oh yes," Ian responded ominously, "I believe I do. And if you think hard enough old friend, I believe that you will, as well."

Tanna's eyes darted back and forth as she racked her brain for an answer. Finally, she looked at Ian and said, "I am at a loss."

"Well, I am sure that our guests from Avalon have a clue," Ian said as he turned to face Averyil and Elwyn. "What do you think? You have a lake, a missing person, and blood and entrails along the water's edge..."

"If I had to venture a guess," Elwyn said slowly, "I would say that all of the indicators suggest a Kelpie..."

"Exactly!" Ian declared.

"What's a Kelpie?" Annalise asked.

"A soulless monster," Tanna said as the color drained from her face. "A cruel, hideous creature that crawled out of someone's nightmares!"

"A Kelpie," Ian explained as he glanced briefly at his friend, "is a evil water spirit – another species of shape-shifter. More often than not it takes on the form of a large black horse; but it has been known to take on a human guise, as well.

"Generally, they are found near bodies of water – they are water spirits, so that goes without saying – and it is there that they lay in wait for their victims; luring them to their deaths."

"How do they do that?" Zoe asked nervously.

"They say," Averyil chimed in, "that a Kelpie, while in their horse form, is one of the most beautiful animals one will ever lay eyes upon. Large, and powerfully built, it is a majestic beast with a shiny ebony coat. It has a long, flowing mane; and eyes that seem to peer into your very soul."

"Yes," Ian agreed, "you are drawn to it – like a moth to the flame. Inevitably, the victim will almost always climb onto the creature's back of their own free will, and once they do that their fate is sealed. The Kelpie will charge into the water where it drowns its victim, later devouring them and discarding the hapless person's bowels on the shore."

"Holy crap...," Erik croaked, "...Mike!"

"Can't you just jump off of the thing and swim to safety?" Angelica asked even though she was sure that she already knew the answer.

"Once your flesh makes contact with that of a Kelpie," Elwyn replied, "you are trapped. You are only free when the beast releases you, and it only releases you in order to feed upon you."

"That's gross!" Zoe declared.

"I need you to think, Erik," Ian said as he walked over to the boy and placed his hands upon his shoulders. "Did you observe anything out of place while you were at the lake? Anything unusual?"

"You mean like a horse?" Erik asked, still shaken by the thought of his good friend's grisly end.

"No, no...," Ian said softly, "...remember, the Kelpie can also assume a human form!"

"I...I don't know," Erik said slowly. "There were police officers all over the place!"

"Other than the two investigative officers," Ian continued urgently, "were there any others that paid an inordinate amount of attention to you or Zoe?"

"There was one guy," Zoe answered. Everyone turned and looked at her. "He was poking around the grass looking for evidence, I guess."

"What was it that drew your attention to him?" Ian asked hastily.

"Well," Zoe said, "I just assumed that he had been wading around the shallow part of the lake because he wasn't wearing any shoes..."

"Yes, yes...," Ian said, "...go on!"

"But the weird thing was his hair," Zoe continued. "It was dripping wet, but his clothing was dry."

"Where did you see this man?" Ian asked, concerned.

"H...he was standing not too far away from Erik and me," she said, "right after Mr. Hedley left us."

"I remember now," Erik said, "we were talking about coming back here to tell you and Tanna what we had learned." He looked over at Ian. "Do you think...?"

"That he was listening to everything that you two said," Ian cut in, "yes, I do. And if that is indeed the case, then it is almost a certainty that Morgan is not only aware of my presence here in Traverse City, but she knows my exact location, as well. The Kelpie must be an agent of hers."

"But why would you assume that?" Blair asked.

"Unless there are other unholy creatures in this city in search of human flesh why would he not?" Elwyn said sarcastically before looking at Erik. "Present company excluded, of course."

"A Kelpie is just the type of creature that Morgan would employ to keep an eye on Erik," Tanna said with a dour tone.

"Yes," Ian agreed. "A Kelpie has the one characteristic that would make it unique for a mission such as this. It cannot be detected by demons – it puts off no discernable scent."

"She sent it to spy on *me*?" Erik asked. "Why?"

"I fear she may have surmised the location of the Book," Ian confessed.

"What are you saying?" Zoe asked as she looked anxiously from Erik to Ian. "Is Erik in danger from this Kelpie?"

"My dear," Ian replied, "if what I suspect is true; you, me, the others – even your families – are all in danger now."

"Do you really think that she would send that...thing...to harm our families?" Eryn asked, trembling.

"This is Morgan le Fay we are talking about," Ian said. "Knowing her, that Kelpie could be just one of the many evils that she has in her little bag of tricks!"

"Are you trying to be cute?" Eryn cried as her voice grew louder. "Do you think that this is some kind of a joke?!" She looked around the room at the stunned faces of her friends. "I can't believe any of this! I can't believe that you guys are just standing here listening to this! This is never going to stop no matter what we do!"

"Eryn," Tanna said softly as she made her way over to the frightened girl, "it will be all right. If we remain calm we can…"

"NO!" Eryn yelled as she backed away. "I'm tired of this! Magic books, man-eating Kelpies – we've put our families in danger, don't you see that?!"

Eryn made her way to the back door and turned to look back at the others. "I don't give a crap about what the rest of you decide to do. My mom is all that I have in this world and I plan on making sure that she is safe!" With that, Eryn winked from view.

"Well," Ian confessed numbly, "I wasn't expecting *that!*"

"So what *are* we going to do?" Annalise demanded. "I won't stand by and let Morgan hurt my family, either!"

"There's only one thing that we can do," Ian said as he looked around the room. "We are going to have to take your families somewhere safe, but there is something that must be done before we hide them away. We all, each of us, owe them something."

"What do you mean," Erik asked, "what do we owe them?"

"The truth, my boy. It is time to tell them the truth."

"You mean about us?!" Zoe asked in disbelief. "But why? Why, after all of this time?"

"Because," Ian answered, "we need to return to Avalon, and I think it only fair that they be allowed to understand why."

"We're going *back* to Avalon?" Blair asked.

"Yes. The key to Erik's plight, as well as the safety of our two worlds, has been hidden there by Merlin; and we need to find it before Morgan learns of its existence."

* * *

Sims sat as still as a statue as he peered out of the darkened windows of the SUV at the house directly across from him. Notebook in his lap, he adjusted the parabolic microphone in order to eradicate some of the static that marred the conversation he was attempting to eavesdrop on. The information concerning the Kelpie intrigued him, and he made a mental note to read up on this mysterious creature later.

The buzzing of his cell phone on the car's dashboard momentarily pulled him away from Ian discussing the relocation of the girls' parents, and reaching out, he saw that it was Eagler's name on the screen. He was just about to answer the phone when Ian said something that caused him to take notice. Tossing the phone onto the seat beside him, he blew off the phone call as he turned the microphone's volume up and pressed one of the headphones closer to his ear.

He listened intently as Ian discussed they're having to return to Avalon – and the reason behind the return trip caused his eyebrows to flare upward in surprise. Sims concentrated on the conversation within the Solorio house for a few moments longer; firmly convinced that he did indeed hear Ian say what he thought he had said. He

removed his headphones and reached for his phone —
quickly finding Eagler's number on speed dial.

"Hey," he said when his partner picked up, "it's me.
I'm at the Solorio house..." There was some angry
grumbling from the other end of the line before Sims
continued. "Well, how was I supposed to know that you
had talked to her?! Listen, I'm coming to the station...you
need to hear this." There was a pause as he was
interrupted by his friend. "What?" Sims barked as Eagler's
muffled question was repeated. "Oh yeah...it's *real*
interesting! I'll see you in a few minutes." He shut the
phone down and tossed it back onto the passenger seat.

"Going on a little scavenger hunt, are you?" he said
as he glanced over at the house. "Well, you better hope
that you find it before Morgan does!"

*   *   *

Eryn barreled into the kitchen, her tennis shoes
sliding across the tile floor as she came to a screeching halt.
She wasted no time in reverting back to her human form
before calling out to her mother — a frantic tone in her

voice. Elisa hurried into the room; the sound of her daughter's voice immediately putting her on alert.

"Honey," she said quickly as she took in her child's harried state, "are you okay? What's wrong?!"

"N-nothing," Eryn said apologetically. "I...I just got a little freaked out when I didn't see you in the kitchen – you're always in the kitchen around this time!"

Elisa looked Eryn over appraisingly. "I was putting some things away in the other room...are you *sure* there's nothing wrong?"

"Nothing that you would understand," Eryn said sadly as she slumped onto a stool alongside the island, "or could even help me with, for that matter..."

"Oh I don't know," her mother said as she sat down beside her, "try me. I don't profess to have the answers to all of life's problems, but I *am* a pretty good listener. Sometimes, that's all we really need – someone to just listen..."

Eryn sighed heavily as she looked at her mother, her eyes welling with tears. "What would you say if I told you that I'm not what you think I am...?"

"Well that's easy," Elisa said with a smile, "you're a talented, kind, loving, intelligent, and beautiful young woman – why I was just telling Janet Tucker down at the market the other day that…"

"No," Eryn said as her tears rolled down her cheeks, "what I mean is: I'm not *what* you think I am!" Before she had time to think about her actions and change her mind, Eryn transformed back into her Sidhe form. She sat there, her face wet with tears, convinced that her mother was about to bolt from the room in terror.

"I…I d-don't understand…," Elisa said, frightened for her child. Her eyes never left her daughter's as she reached out and took the girl's hands in her own.

"It's a long story…," Eryn said softly. She began to smile as her mother gently wiped the tears from her cheeks.

"Well," Elisa said soothingly, "I suggest you start at the beginning."

6. A Time for Truth

Jeremy threw the car into park and leaned back heavily into his seat. He stared out the windshield at the house sitting in front of him as a grunt of pure disdain crawled from his throat. He was quite proud of the fact that he had maintained a discreet distance from the place for over a year; having been told that he needed to return sickened him.

His wife, Danni, looked over at him and smiled. She realized what coming here did to him emotionally, but their daughter had requested it. Danni knew that he would never disappoint their daughter, but even she had to admit that the invitation had come out of the blue, and Annalise's insistence that they come to the Hedley home immediately was puzzling, to say the least.

"I can't believe that I am actually back here after all of this time," Jeremy whined as he continued to look out at the house that sat looming before him. "I swear Danni, chewing on a mouthful of nails sounds like more fun than being here right now!"

"Oh stop it, you big baby!" Danni scolded her husband. She slapped his knee playfully. "It really wasn't that bad the last time we were here," she said, referring to their visit all those many months ago.

Jeremy, Danni, and Annalise had been invited to the Hedley house for dinner by Erik's father, Junior. His wife, Laura Hedley, was very warm and gracious, if not a little clingy; while Erik, to Annalise's surprise, turned out to be affable and kind. Junior had been the exception. Boisterous and overbearing, he had made them all feel uncomfortable from the moment that they had arrived. The only thing that seemed to have helped in quieting him down was the surprise visit by Ian Rimmel. Junior had spent the best part of the evening glowering at his uninvited guest suspiciously.

None of them were aware that Junior had been under the control of Morgan le Fay. He had arranged the invitation of Annalise's family to his home in order to capture a picture of her and his son alone together. Later, Morgan was to use the photo to make Zoe Beckford jealous – the plan being to destroy the budding friendship amongst the girls. Ian's unannounced arrival had ruined all of that.

"You're kidding me, right?" Jeremy asked as he looked over at his wife.

"Okay, okay!" she said, giving up on her attempt at mollifying him. "Excuse me for trying to put a positive spin on things. But technically we aren't here to see Junior — our *daughter* asked us to come."

"Yeah," Jeremy observed with a hint of confusion in his voice, "I still haven't figured that one out." As he and his wife climbed out of their car he glanced at the police cruiser that was parked in front of the house. "And I wonder why *that* is here?"

"Do you think it has anything to do with the missing person investigation that we saw on the news?" Danni asked nervously.

"It's hard to say," Jeremy answered. "Whatever the reason, I'm sure it involves Junior somehow." He took his wife by the hand and gave it a squeeze before leading her toward the house. As they crossed the graveled drive, another car pulled up and parked alongside their SUV. Rick and Barb Beckford, Zoe's parents, got out of the car and waved at Jeremy and Danni. The look of relief on Jeremy's face made his wife laugh out loud.

"Boy, are you two a sight for sore eyes!" Jeremy said as he grabbed Rick's hand and gave it a shake. "For a moment there, I thought I was going to have to endure the company of the great Junior Hedley all alone!"

"You can have him!" Rick said, laughing. *"We're* here because we got a really strange phone call from Zoe."

"Really?" Danni asked, her curiosity piqued. "We received a similar phone call from Annalise. Any idea what's going on?"

"Not a clue," Barb answered, "but Mister over-protective here swore up and down that it had something to do with Erik."

"Well, have you seen the way he looks at our daughter?" Rick said before laughing along with the others. The moment came to an abrupt end, however, when yet another car came up the driveway. The sedan eased to a stop, and as Tim Wagner shut off the engine his wife, Cassie, stepped out of the passenger side of the vehicle.

"Okay," Jeremy said as Blair's parents approached them, "things have officially gotten weird."

"Let me guess," Tim said as he looked at everyone assembled in the driveway, "mysterious phone call from each of your girls asking you to meet them here at the Hedley house. What's going on?"

"Perhaps I can answer that question for you," Ian said as he came walking out of the front door; followed closely by Erik, his mother and father, and Chief Whipple.

Jeremy looked up at his old friend standing on the porch with the Hedleys and smiled, but he found it difficult to shake the feeling of déjà vu. "Ian," he said while trying not to appear surprised, "long time, no see! What are *you* doing here?"

"Hold on a minute," Barb said as she looked from Ian to her husband, and then at Jeremy, "what did you call him?"

"Ian Rimmel," Danni said, answering for her husband. "He's an old personal friend of ours from way back."

"I'm not sure *who* Ian Rimmel is," Rick said as he stared at the man on the front porch, "but we *do* know *him*! His name is Archer...Archer Conroy; he helped us through our adoption process with Zoe. That was years ago of course, but that was something – he's someone – you just don't forget!"

Ian stepped down from the porch and walked across the gravel path toward the Wagoners. As he grew closer, Cassie, trembling slightly, retreated into her husband's arms. She stared at him, gobsmacked, as he looked at her, and then her husband.

"You remember me as well, don't you, Tim? Cassie?" He paused for a moment. "When we last met I was calling myself Edwin Doyle..."

"How do you forget the man that handed you your daughter?" Tim said, his voice shaky. "The last time we saw you, we were leaving the adoption agency with Blair..."

"Yes," Ian said quietly as he nodded his head.

"What, exactly, is going on here, Ian?" Jeremy demanded as he and Danni, as well as the others, gathered around him. Ian could see the anger and confusion in his friends eyes. "How could you have possibly been involved with *each* of our adoptions?"

"You had better be very careful with what you are about to say," Pete Whipple said as he pushed his way past the huddled group of perplexed parents. "These people deserve some answers, but I swear to you that if I can determine that you have committed a crime – regardless of the jurisdiction – I will arrest you here and now!"

"C'mon guys," Erik pleaded, "give him a chance to explain!"

"You stay out of this, son!" Junior said. He had always suspected that the man standing before him had, from the very moment that he had met him, been up to no good. Now he had a front row seat to Ian's likely downfall, and he did not want to miss a thing.

"I really hope that you can explain yourself, Ian!" Danni said as her eyes began to well up. "How does one man, with three different identities, assist in three separate adoptions without something not being on the up and up? Were any of these adoptions even legal?!"

"Please," Ian said quickly; the panic and desperation in Danni's voice stabbing him in the heart like a knife, "all of you, please! If you would just give me one moment to explain I hope to make everything clear to you all."

Finally, they all grew quiet. The intensity of their stares cut across him like highly focused lasers. Ian looked at each of them in turn; dejected by what he was now doing to them. They were good, decent people – it was why he had chosen them to raise and protect the girls – who did not deserve what was currently happening to them. The time had come, however, to do what was necessary. He knew that he was tearing their worlds apart, and the knowledge of it was eating him up inside.

"None of this is going to be easy to understand," he said slowly, "but before I go on I must stress one thing. I want to assure each of you that the child that you adopted is indeed your daughter! Nothing will ever change that. Ever!

"There are, however, certain circumstances that have arisen concerning the girls and young Erik here, that require me to now reveal to you the truth about them. Truths that I don't think any of you are going to find easy to understand *or* believe, but truths they are, nonetheless."

"Erik...?" Laura Hedley stammered as she stared at Ian glassy-eyed. "I don't understand; what about my Erik?"

"A moment, madam, if you please." Ian cleared his throat before continuing. "I have a confession to make. As you all have come to realize, I am not exactly who I have purported myself to be. I am not Archer Conroy or Edwin Doyle – or Ian Rimmel for that matter..."

"Who are you, then?" Junior demanded to know.

"My name is Merlin."

They all stared at him wide-eyed. "M-merlin who?" Pete Whipple asked warily.

"That's all that there is," he said. "Merlin. Simply Merlin."

"Merlin," Jeremy said slowly, "as in the wizard? King Arthur and his knights. That Merlin?"

"The one and the same, I'm afraid."

"I knew it," Junior said incredulously, "this guy is a certifiable nutcase!"

"I don't know about the rest of you," Rick said incensed, "but I have had enough of this crap! You tell me where my daughter is *right* now or so help me...!"

"Yes," Merlin said. He had expected this reaction and was prepared for what was coming next. "I see that I am going to have to prove myself to you all. So be it – let's bring the girls out, shall we?"

Merlin stepped away from everyone, out toward the center of the gravel drive, and then turned to Erik and nodded his head. Erik, waiting for his cue, nodded as well before summoning up the portal. As the doorway between space and time opened up, Jeremy and the other parents all took involuntary steps backward. The stench of ozone burned their noses, and Erik watched, concerned, as his mother fell against his father for support. Junior held onto her, unable to pull his eyes away from what was happening right in front of him.

"What in the world...?" Jeremy whispered. He was finding it hard to believe that he was actually seeing what was occurring before his very eyes, but he found it even harder still when he saw shapes emerging from within the distortion's murky well.

Out of the rift stepped Tanna, followed by Zoe, Blair, Annalise, and Angelica. Several seconds after they stepped out of the portal, Elwyn and Averyil exited. The two warriors stood there, carefully scrutinizing the girls' parents who were staring back at them in shock, as the portal closed behind them with a loud pop.

Merlin walked over and took his place with the girls and their companions. He had taken note that Tanna had decided to arrive in her natural form. The fact that she was no longer hiding her true appearance pleased him. He took in the expressions on the faces of Jeremy, Danni, and the others – shock, fear, confusion – and then cleared his throat again, drawing their attention reluctantly back to him.

"Here they are," Merlin said with a flourish. "Safe and sound!"

"No, no, no, NO!" Morgan shrieked as she stormed about the room. She was raking her fingers through her hair, leaving it fiercely disheveled. "Why, in the name of the four realms, would they be going *back* to Avalon? Their return will seriously jeopardize everything that I have put into motion!"

She paced the floor a few moments longer before turning to face Sims and Eagler. Her features were strained, and her eyes were black with anger. "You heard nothing more – when they were leaving; or the reason for their going?"

Eagler stared straight ahead while Sims continued with his report. He explained to Morgan that he had remained outside the house until he observed the girls exiting the back door and walking out into the yard. Each one of them was on a cell phone; and from what he could gather through the microphone's static, they were all calling their parents.

"The mike wasn't working as well as I had hoped," Sims went on, "There was a lot of interference..."

"Did you hear anything or not, you fool?!" Morgan screeched.

"There was talk about returning to find something that Merlin – the one that you thought you had destroyed – had hidden. The Rimmel guy mentioned a staff..."

Morgan's mood changed immediately as her eyes bulged wide at this latest revelation. "Did you say a *staff*? You are quite certain that you heard him say that he needed to locate a *staff*?"

"Yes," Sims said nodding his head. "Rimmel said that they would need the staff."

"Need it? Need it for what...?" Morgan pressed.

"I'm not sure," Sims answered. "That's when the static kicked in big time, but right after that he was talking about that book that you have been searching for."

Morgan stood quietly for a spell – her mind dancing about from all of the implications that this new bit of information held. She puzzled through it, trying to determine what Merlin was up to. Her eyes finally lit up when she surmised what she believed to be the only possible answer.

"He needs the staff in order to access the Book of E'lythmarium!" she claimed excitedly. "That is the only possible explanation that makes any sense. That means," she said as she took a seat, "that he will *have* the Book in his possession when he returns to Avalon!"

"That would be my guess," Eagler agreed, and then he looked over at his partner. "But why take the kids? What purpose would they serve?"

"Beats me," Sims said. "But I also heard them discussing the parents. Apparently, they fear for their safety and were making plans to hide them away until they got back."

"Over my dead body!" Morgan snarled as she jumped back onto her feet. "I swore that the Elementals would suffer, and part of that entails the demise of each, and every one, of their family members. I promised those brats that I would get even with them and I intend to see that through!"

"What do you plan to do, Mistress?" Eagler asked.

"I will summon Malo," Morgan hissed, "and then he and I will return to Avalon. I must locate the staff before Merlin can get his hands on it. I will need the two of you to take care of a *very* important task for me while I am away…"

The two men stared at her, waiting and ready to do her bidding.

"I need you to locate the families; and when you find them, kill them. Kill them all. I want them to die a slow, agonizing death!"

Eagler stood there, his fists tightly clenched; while Sims slowly, and imperceptibly, shook his head back and forth. She watched, annoyed, as the two men struggled with her latest request. Morgan could feel them fighting with all of their might, trying once again to break free of her hold over them. This latest command went against every fiber of their being – it was contrary to all that they stood for – and their minds rebelled against it.

Morgan pushed back against their growing disobedience until their minds were completely hers once more. She desperately needed them to do this for her – she was unsure if she would be able to return to do it herself; so to soften the blow, she provided them with an inducement, something that would make the task more palatable to their pained psyches.

"Do this, this *last* thing for me," she purred, "and you will be free of me, forever. On this, you have my word!"

Eagler and Sims stood silently for an instant looking at one another with their large black eyes before they turned to face Morgan. "Yes, Mistress...," they answered before turning and leaving the cabin.

*　*　*

Merlin tried to explain the history of the Sidhe, and their relationship to the girls, as best as he could, but he found himself running headlong into their parents growing skepticism. Finally, frustrated by the cynicism and suspicious accusations, he asked the girls to revert to their natural state. Their transformations had the desired effect. Now, there were a slew of questions, and he did his best to answer them all. He attempted to explain himself and the reasoning behind all of his actions, but he could tell, through all of the tears and the looks of betrayal, that they no longer trusted him. When, in the end, he tried to reach out to Jeremy and Danni, they both pulled away; and he knew that things would never be the same between them again.

By this time, everyone had retreated to the house. Luara had felt self-conscious out in the open, and wanted to remove the spectacle that was playing out in front of them away from prying eyes. There was, of course, no one around for miles – they had sent all of their employees home earlier that day – but she could not help but feel as though they were being watched.

They were all seated in the Hedleys' great room – the girls huddled up alongside their parents, while Erik and his family stood quietly beside a large, white Steinway piano. Merlin and Tanna stood in the center of the room, while Elwyn and Averyil had withdrawn to a back corner so they could observe what was unfolding before them. The two warriors eyed each of the adoptive parents silently – marveling at the fact that, although their worlds had just been turned upside down, the love that they felt for their daughters was undeniable. It was as if the girls had not changed in their eyes at all. No matter who, or what these girls were, to these humans they were their children, and they would never let them go.

A noise from the outer corridor caused them all to freeze in place, as a palpable fear gripped the room. Chief

Whipple motioned for quiet as he got up to see what was going on. The parents all eyed each other anxiously, pulling their children close to them as Merlin looked at the doorway where Whipple had disappeared gravely. It was not long before the police chief returned, and Eryn and her mother, Elisa, followed in his wake. Merlin was about to breathe a sigh of relief when the woman stormed past the bewildered officer, marched right up to the wizard, and slapped him across the face.

"How dare you, Adrian?!" she barked as she glared angrily at the stunned, but silent sorcerer.

"He's, uh, going by Merlin now," Jeremy offered before his wife elbowed him in the side.

"I don't care what he's calling himself these days," Elisa snapped as she continued to stare at Merlin, "he put my baby – our babies – in danger, and didn't even have the stomach to inform us of his actions! No, instead, he placed us all under some sort of *spell* and whisked them away to who knows where! What would you have done if something had happened to one of them – erased our memory? What kind of monster *are* you?"

"I," Merlin stammered meekly, "I would never have let...,"

"Please," Elisa said as she turned her back on him, "don't speak to me right now!"

"So," Jeremy said as he tried to change the mood of the discussion, "I read stories about Elementals when I was a kid. All of them gave the impression that Elementals, and beings like Tanna here, are immortal. You're not telling us that our kids are going to live forever," he said as he looked into Annalise's silvery-white eyes, "are you?"

"Not exactly," Annalise answered as she held her father's hand tightly.

"Their lifespan *will* be substantially longer than yours," Elwyn said gruffly.

"Just how old are *you*?" Rick asked Elwyn, curious.

"I am three cycles old as of this past month," the prince answered.

"Three cycles...?"

"Sidhe children age just as human children do," Tanna explained, "until their eighteenth year. At that point, they begin to age in what we call cycles."

"And how do you measure a cycle?" Danni asked.

"It's approximately eighteen years," Merlin responded. "Give or take."

"So, for every eighteen of *our* years…," Elisa whispered as she looked at Eryn.

"Your daughters will age one cycle," Merlin said.

Danni looked at each of the Sidhe before addressing Tanna. "So, how old are you – if you don't mind my asking."

"Not at all," Tanna said. "I am upon my sixty-fifth cycle."

"T-that," Danni said shocked, "would make you…"

"A little over eleven hundred years old!" Tim gasped.

"One thousand one hundred and seventy," Tanna smiled, "to be exact."

"That's incredible!" Junior said.

"I have a question," Laura said nervously, not sure if she really wanted an answer, "but what does any of this have to do with my Erik? He was not adopted – he's our own flesh and blood! He isn't a Sidhe…"

"No," Erik said to his mother as he took her hands in his, "I'm not a Sidhe, but there is something that you need to know about me."

"What is it, son?" Junior asked as he placed his hand on Erik's shoulder. "What do we need to know about you?"

"I've become...," Erik gulped nervously, "I've become a..."

"A warlock," Merlin said loudly.

"A...what?" Junior asked, dumbfounded.

"A warlock," Merlin said again, "and a rather good one if I must say so myself!"

"Magical powers. Wizards and castles. I'm sorry, but this is all a bit much!" Cassie declared, echoing Eryn's sentiments from earlier in the day. Blair gave her mom a hug as her father put his arms around them both.

Barb looked at them for a moment before she turned to Averyil. "So, it's true then, that Zoe and Annalise are twins, and you are their older sister?"

"Yes," Averyil said, "that is correct. Outside of the three of us, and our grandfather, we are all that are left of our family."

"Well," Danni said as she looked at the three girls, "I would hope that you could consider each of us as family from now on..."

"I would be honored to consider you all a part of my family," Averyil said, smiling warmly.

"The House of Alron would gladly welcome Blair's family as well," Elwyn said, glancing at Tim and his wife.

"Not in this lifetime!" Tim barked.

"I beg your pardon," Elwyn said as everyone in the room stared at them.

"If I understood the tale that Merlin told us earlier," Tim began angrily, "you and your brother – Lathos, is it? – have it in for my Blair! There's no way on this earth that I will ever..."

"And as *I* believe Merlin has already explained," Elwyn said loudly, "I was bewitched! Bewitched, I might add, by the same odious creature that means to do *you* all harm!"

"Let me guess," Jeremy chuckled as he made an attempt at easing the tension in the room, " The evil sorceress Morgan le Fay is out to get us!" When he saw his daughter and her friends grow stony-faced he slumped into

his seat wide-eyed. "I...I'm *joking*, here! W-wait a minute
– are you telling me that...that she's for *real*?!"

"Very much so, I'm afraid." Merlin confirmed. "That
is why I had no choice but to reveal all of this to you. It is
because of her, and the threat that she poses to our two
worlds, that you all must go into hiding!"

"Now wait just a minute," Pete Whipple said as he
got out of his chair. He had listened to all of this
awestruck, not only by Merlin's fantastic story but by the
amazing transformation of the girls that he had witnessed.
"A lady by the name of Morgan came by my station just the
other day wanting my help in trying to locate you..."

"Yes," Merlin nodded. "That was Morgan le Fay."

"You expect me to believe that that wisp of a woman
could be considered some kind of threat?" Pete objected.

"Obviously Chief," Merlin countered, "you would not
remember how evil she truly is."

"Remember...?" Pete said. "What are you talking
about? I only just met the woman a few days ago!"

"Is that so?" Merlin said as he walked over to where
the police chief stood. "Then you won't mind if I show you
something?"

"Show me what?" Pete demanded.

Merlin stuck his hand into his pocket and pulled it right back out again, his fist clenched tight. "You may want to have a look at this too, Mr. Hedley. I believe that you will find it interesting, as well."

Junior walked over apprehensively and stood beside his friend; not quite sure that he *wanted* to see what Merlin had in his possession, but his curiosity got the better of him.

Merlin opened his hand, revealing a small green stone the size of an acorn. He held the stone between his thumb and index finger, holding it up for the two men to inspect. As they stared at the trinket, it began to glow warmly. Gradually, as the light within it intensified, their eyes grew fixed. In that instant, for Junior and Pete, the room and its occupants seemed to fade away; and the only presence with them now was that of Merlin's voice repeating one word again and again.

"Remember...!"

Without warning, a deluge of memories washed over them like a flood. Feelings, sensations, sounds and smells assailed their minds – whisking them both back to the terrible deeds that they had committed more than a year ago. Transgressions that Merlin had hidden from them in order to maintain the normalcy of their lives were now laid bare, and it hit them like a ton of bricks.

"Oh my God!" Chief Whipple whispered hoarsely as the color drained from his face. He took several plodding steps before he collapsed onto the sofa. While the dark recollections continued to roil within his head, the frightful images dealt Junior a much harder blow.

Erik ran to his father as the man fell to his knees. His gut-wrenching sobs pulling at the very heartstrings of everyone in the room. To see this man, who wore his masculinity on his sleeve brought to this, it was though all of the air was being sucked out of the room.

"My boy!" he wailed as he wrapped his arms around his son's waist. "My boy – I never meant to...meant to...!" His words dropped off as his body was wracked with grief. Erik, overcome himself by his father's display, held him tightly as tears fell down his own cheeks. In that moment, father and son knew the truth about one another, and a doorway to true friendship and forgiveness had finally opened.

Rick cleared his throat, but the emotions brought about by what he had just witnessed could still be heard in his voice. "You may not know these families very well, Merlin, but I do. It's going to take a lot more than a ghost story about some witch to prevent any of us from staying right here and protecting our kids!"

"No," Pete said, "that's where you're wrong! Trust me when I tell you that these are more than just *ghost stories*, my friend! That woman is evil – I mean pure evil! She will do unspeakable things to you; all of you. But first, she will take whoever you hold dear and make you watch as they suffer – and mark my words, they *will* suffer!"

"What are we going to do?!" Elisa blurted out.

"Please, calm down everyone." Merlin said placatingly. "I have a plan that will see you and your families to safety. Tanna will explain it all to you, but you must follow her directions precisely!"

As they all gathered around to hear what Tanna had to say, Merlin stepped over to Chief Whipple. Slipping his arm over the man's shoulder, he lowered his voice to a whisper.

"I'm sure, Chief, that you would appreciate an opportunity to erase away some of your past misdeeds, yes?"

"Right now," Pete said with a trembling voice, "there isn't anything that I *wouldn't* do!"

"That is good to know," Merlin continued, "and extremely important if my plan is to go off without a hitch."

"What do you need me to do?"

"You have two officers – a Captain Sims and a Captain Eagler – in your employ, do you not?"

"Yeah," Pete said confused. "But I don't see what they..."

Merlin took the man's hand in his and gripped it firmly. "Now, Chief Whipple," he said as he looked him in the eye, "listen to me very carefully..."

*   *   *

Sims walked into Eagler's office and stopped at the edge of the desk, looking down at his partner as the man scribbled notes onto a piece of paper. "Ready to go?" he asked.

"Just about," Eagler said as he glanced at the monitor of his PC. "Let me get this last address and then we can hit it."

"What we are about to do is wrong," Sims said tightly.

"I know," Eagler agreed. He could feel Morgan's grip on him weakening, but he still felt compelled to complete this last grisly task. "That's why I plan on turning myself in when it's done."

"Already typed out my confession," Sims said. "She still has my mind – I can feel her inside my head, but I won't let her take my soul!"

Both men stopped talking when they heard a noise at the door. They turned and looked at Chief Whipple; their eyes still concealed behind their sunglasses.

"Help you, Chief?" Eagler asked.

"Yeah," Pete said amiably, "you two got a minute?"

"We were just about to hit the road," Sims said.

"Oh," the older man said as he closed the door behind him, "this will only take a minute. There's something that I think you guys ought to see."

"What is it?" Eagler asked gruffly.

"This," Pete said as he held up the tiny green stone that Merlin had passed to him. As the rock's inner light grew more acute, the two officers in front of him froze in place – their eyes locked onto the gem. When he was sure that they were completely under the stone's power, he uttered the word that he was instructed to repeat five times.

"Forget...!"

7. The Cottage in the Northern Woods

Thalthas made his way down the corridor; his footfalls echoing loudly throughout the cold, anemic hallway. He ignored the portraits, tapestries, and statuary that, in the past , would usually have brought out a deeply rooted sense of reverence and pride in him as he made his way to the throne room. All of the dazzling pieces of art had now lost their meaning. Since the tragic death of King Alron and the subsequent imprisonment of Queen Nionia, Castle Thoron had lost the spark that had once made it a bastion of integrity, benevolence, and peace. Now, it felt like a crude distortion of its former self – a place of gloom and dismay.

The guards posted outside of the throne room took note of him as he approached, pulling themselves to attention. Thalthas ignored the sentries as he pushed the massive doors open and proceeded into the great hall. As he entered the room he could see that Lathos was not alone. Someone, who was wearing a thick long cloak with the hood pulled over their head to hide their features, stood near the king.

Once again, Lathos was holding court with the one person whom he seemed to trust above all of his other advisors. Not since the passing of his father had any one individual held so much sway over Lathos as this one seemed to. Thalthas ignored the visitor and walked up to the throne, bowing his head slightly when the king finally took notice of him.

"You sent for me, my lord." Thalthas' voice was flat as it echoed slightly in the large room.

"Yes, Thalthas, I did." Lathos said as he acknowledged the commanding general of his army. "It has been brought to my attention that Merlin is on his way to Avalon."

"Merlin?" Thalthas said confused. "But I was under the impression from your majesty's earlier statements that the old warlock was dead..."

"That was my impression as well at the time," Lathos muttered as he glared at the visitor under the hood anew. "It appears that the reports we received were spurious, at best. Be that as it may," he said turning to Thalthas once more, "it now seems that he is on his way here – to Castle Thoron. I would like him intercepted."

"Intercepted, my lord? Where would I even begin to look for him?"

"Yes," Lathos answered. "Think for a moment. If you were Merlin, and you believed that everyone thought you were dead — and you wanted them to continue to believe so — where would you go to keep out of sight?"

"The cottage in the Northern Woods," Thalthas said absently.

"Yes, exactly! The residence provided to him by Alron. Take a team of Riders and see if you can verify that he is indeed there."

"May I be so bold as to ask where you might have obtained this...latest bit of information, lord?" Thalthas inquired as he scowled at the King's cowled visitant.

"Where I obtained my information is of no consequence to you, Thalthas. All I require from you is that you gather up your men and make haste to the cottage."

"And if we should find him there, your highness?"

"If you *do* find him," Lathos said brusquely, "I want you to escort him back to Castle Thoron. Bring him to me personally. Is that clear, Thalthas?"

"Yes, your highness." Thalthas acknowledged as he bowed his head. "I will leave immediately."

Lathos watched impassively as Thalthas turned on his heel and left the room. When the large wooden doors shut noisily behind him, the newly crowned King of Gorias got up from his throne chair and stormed past Morgan le Fay in a huff.

"I seriously cannot believe that you allowed Merlin to slip through your fingers yet again. After all that we have accomplished – this is outrageous!"

"He did not *slip* through my fingers," Morgan growled as she pulled the hood from over her head. "You need to watch your tone, Lathos!"

"That is *King* Lathos," he sneered as he turned to face the sorceress, "and what would you call his miraculous return to the land of the living? You told me that he was dead – that you had killed him yourself!"

"I assumed that I had!" Morgan snapped as she returned Lathos' icy stare. "I was just as shocked as you are now when I learned that he had created a doppelganger."

"Doppleganger...?" Lathos echoed.

"Yes," Morgan explained. "It seems that the old goat could not afford to leave Avalon when he learned of the Shadow King's reach, but his precious Elementals were also in need of him at the time. So, out of desperation, he utilized a spell that essentially split him into two individual beings. He allowed the copy to go and see to the Elementals while he remained here to assist your father."

"Then if the man that you killed was truly Merlin," Lathos said hopefully, "we have nothing to fear! This...copy...is merely an imposter."

"Not quite," Morgan went on. "In essence, when Merlin split himself in two, there existed not one, but *two* Merlins. They were the same man, with the same abilities – albeit weaker. Two halves of a whole, you might say."

"So when you dispatched the Merlin who had remained here," Lathos pondered aloud, "you, in effect, weakened considerably the Merlin that went off to aid my sister and the others."

"That is correct," Morgan answered, "but just because he is weak is no reason to underestimate him."

"Oh, I agree," Lathos said as he returned to his throne, "but why return to Avalon – especially now?"

"I believe," Morgan said excitedly, "that he has come to retrieve his staff!"

Lathos stared at her questioningly. "His staff? Are you referring to that old piece of wood that he always carried around with him? I was under the impression that he used that to support himself."

"Oh, it is much more than that," Morgan said as she approached the throne, "much more! Merlin channeled his magic through that 'old piece of wood.' My guess is that he needs it now in order to restore his powers."

"So this staff is important...?"

"If I were to locate the staff before Merlin," she said with a gleam in her eye, "he would no longer be a threat!"

"That is all well and good," Lathos said, "but what of the Elementals and that accursed human? What would you do about them?"

Morgan paced slowly back and forth in front of the dais – her thoughts racing through her head as she speculated on her enemies next possible move. Lathos watched her closely as she moved about the room. His faith in her abilities had dampened of late; what with his brother's escape from the dungeons and now this debacle involving the death and resurrection of Merlin. Her quest for the Book of E'lythmarium, as well as her insatiable desire for revenge, was slowly, but surely, putting all of his plans in grave danger of failing. *Perhaps*, Lathos thought to himself, *the time is fast approaching where I will need to rid myself of this witch.*

"Would it be possible," Morgan uttered abruptly, "for you to convene the High Council?"

"The High Council...?" Lathos snorted. "Whatever for?"

Morgan climbed up onto the dais and locked eyes with the king. "With the growing threat that the Elementals and their abhorrent pet represent to our plans it is imperative – now more than ever – that they grant you permission to war on the humans, thereby allowing you to take back the Northern Isles!"

"Have you completely lost control of your senses?!" Lathos asked as he stared at her, appalled. He had, reluctantly, grown accustomed to her speaking to him as an equal, but her taking the dais was a breach of decorum that exceeded even her own hubris. "The High Council would never agree to allow me to attack the humans without provocation – especially at this juncture!"

"If we cannot *make* them see, then we will attack without their permission! Surely your troops..."

"My troops are nowhere near ready," Lathos said as he jumped from the throne and put some distance between himself and Morgan. "I require *at least* another six months before I could even dream of mounting an attack!"

"Yes," Morgan said smiling self-confidently, "but once I have Merlin's staff *and* the Book of E'lythmarium..."

"You and that confounded book!" Lathos lashed out angrily. "Do you not see how this ludicrous crusade of yours is ruining everything that we have accomplished up to now?! Let us first concentrate on destroying the Elementals, ridding ourselves of Merlin and his ill-fated apprentice, and then, when the timing is right, make our move on Avalon and the Northern Isles. We are so close to having it all!"

"And we *shall* have it all," Morgan said as she opened a portal. She made almost no effort whatsoever to hide the fact that she was ignoring him. "You will see; once the Book and Merlin's staff are mine, we will have everything – and more!" With that, Morgan climbed down from the dais and disappeared into the cold blackness of the rift.

Lathos watched as the portal closed behind the sorceress; suddenly aware that he was in league with a mad woman. He hurried over to the throne and pulled on a red velvet sash that extended down from the ceiling. In moments, a servant entered the room from a rear door that was recessed into the wall.

"You sent for me, sire?" the servant said bowing deeply.

"I must speak with Shlogg," Lathos muttered, "tell him that it is urgent!"

*   *   *

There was just enough light from the setting of the sun coming through the window to allow a somewhat cursory inspection of the interior of Merlin's cottage. The dwelling was a rumpled, disheveled mess with all sorts of books, arcane objects, and charts lying about in complete disarray. Chaos seemed to be the theme that he had been going for when, and if, he had decorated the place.

Merlin walked around the room, his expression bereft of any emotion as he glanced t the miscellaneous items scattered all about. Occasionally, he would stop and scrutinize a particular object that had caught his eye, his face alight with recognition, and then he would move on. They all watched him in silence; afraid of breaking his concentration, but after twenty minutes of waiting for a response while he examined each article, Erik could no longer contain himself.

"Do you recognize *anything* in here," he asked as he fidgeted restlessly. "Anything at all?"

Merlin looked over at him; an eyebrow lifted indifferently as he spoke. "I can tell you anything that you want to know about everything within this cottage – its history, where I got it, what they were used for; but *these* hands," he said as he stared at his palms, "have never touched any of them."

"It must be strange," Averyil said as she picked up what appeared to be a snow globe, a tiny house with a small figurine was visible within the sphere, "to have all of these memories, yet knowing that they belong to another."

"Actually," Merlin stated as he walked over to her, "the memories are indeed my own – I just didn't live them." He took the globe from her hands. "And please be careful with this. Tic-Tic hates it when his globe is disturbed. It takes him forever to tidy up his things." Merlin held up the glass ball for Averyil to see, and she gasped when she noticed the tiny figure beside the house shaking a fist at her angrily.

"But you're right," he continued, "it is a bit strange to be here in this place with all of these things that I have collected from all over each of the four realms, but knowing that none of it is truly mine."

"Are your memories such that we can use them to locate your staff?" Tanna asked hopefully.

Merlin sighed as he placed the glass ball back upon its cradle. "Unfortunately, no. Our – mine and Merlin's – memories became our own once the separation spell was employed. I had no insights into his actions, just as he had none into mine."

"So what do we do now?" Eryn asked. It had taken a lot of persuasion, but Merlin and the others had convinced her to accompany them back to Avalon, once they had assured her that her mother would be safe.

"Finding the staff is our main priority," he said as he turned and faced the Elemental. "I will not be able to regain my powers until it, and the Book, are back in my possession."

"So you have figured out a way to separate the book from Erik so he doesn't turn into a crazed monster?" Zoe asked.

"Details, poppet, details…," Merlin said in response, but Zoe held his gaze. "No, I haven't just yet, but I will. I promise!"

"Getting your hands on those things might be *your* priority," Blair said tautly, "but they aren't mine!"

The anger in her voice caused everyone in the room to turn her way. "I beg your pardon?" Merlin said.

"I understand how important the staff is, I really do," Blair's hair began to glow brightly in the dimly lit room, "but there is something that *I* have to do that is just as important!"

Merlin stood silently for a moment before nodding his head. "Yes, I believe that you are quite right, little one. I dare say that it is high time Queen Nionia was freed from her imprisonment."

"I've never been to the dungeons inside Castle Thoron," Blair said, her eyes intense as they scanned the room. "I'm going to need help!"

"And you shall have it," Averyil declared. "I will not rest until Gailon walks free. I will guide you!"

"I'm in," Angelica said.

"Count me in, as well," Elwyn said guiltily. The expression on his face was a somber one. "I owe Gailon a debt that I can never truly repay, and as for Nionia – my mother should no longer have to suffer at the hands of her two wretched sons."

"Perhaps I should accompany them," Tanna said as she walked over to Merlin. "There's no telling what kind of trouble they are liable to get themselves into."

Merlin eyed them all quietly for a moment before nodding his head again. "Agreed. You five will free Queen Nionia and Gailon – I will take the others and continue our search...," he stopped mid-sentence as he turned toward the window.

Sounds from outside the cottage drew their attention, as a muffled growl pulled at Erik's lips – exposing sharp, shiny teeth. His senses heightened, he sniffed at the air before turning to the others.

"Horses!" he murmured harshly. "Everyone get down. Now!"

They all ducked down out of sight as Erik wormed his way over to the window and peeked outside. After a quick inspection, he dropped back down and swung around to face them all.

"There are three men on horseback coming toward the cottage," he said thickly. "One of them looks like Thalthas!"

"How could *he* have known that we would be here?" Zoe asked.

"Morgan le Fay, most likely!" Annalise answered. "But Thalthas is on our side, isn't he? Shouldn't we go out there and meet them?"

"No!" Elwyn hissed. "Lathos most certainly has them out searching for me. If I am seen they will, without a doubt, return me to him!" He glanced over at Averyil. "You will be arrested as well, for your part in my escape!"

"You're correct, of course," Merlin whispered, "but I think that *someone* should go out there. We won't know for sure what is going on unless we speak to Thalthas. If we stay in here, we run the risk of all three coming inside. I, for one, am not comfortable with that."

"I'll go," Erik volunteered. "If things get ugly I'll just invite my friend to the party." Merlin nodded in agreement, and Erik stood up and slipped out the door.

The horses became aware of his presence well before their riders. Their agitated neighing instantly alerted the men to Erik's approach. Nearly in unison, they all pulled harshly on their reins and brought their mounts to a stop. Two of the warriors eyed the young apprentice warily, as the lead rider urged his horse forward. Erik was quick to notice the flicker of surprise in Thalthas' eyes as he made his way toward the cottage. Erik also picked up on Thalthas' subtle message of warning as the warrior gestured slightly in the direction of his companions.

"Well," Thalthas called out as though speaking to someone other than Erik, "it is the young sorcerer in training. Some time has passed since last we met."

"How are you, Thalthas?" Erik asked. "Something I can help you with?"

Thalthas climbed down from his horse and walked over to Erik cautiously. It was more than evident that the boy was safeguarding something or someone. "I seek an audience with the old mage – is he here with you?"

"'The *old* mage'?" Erik asked cagily. "To tell you the truth, it's been a while since I saw *him* last. As a matter of fact," he continued, "I was just on my way to look for him myself!"

"Splendid," Thalthas said as he placed a hand upon Erik's shoulder, "then we shall search for your teacher together." He looked past Erik, to the cottage that had been Merlin's home. "Before we go, do you mind if I take a look inside?"

"Why are you looking for him?" Erik asked, his tone suspicious.

"I will not lie to you," Thalthas answered. "I have been sent by King Lathos to locate, and return with, the old wizard. It is the belief of some whom hold sway over the king that Merlin is here. I ask you, as a friend, to allow me to verify whether or not that is indeed the case."

Erik looked back at the cottage before locking eyes with Thalthas once more. "I *could* stop you, you know."

"I am well aware of that," Thalthas acknowledged.

"If the old man is not here," one of the Rider's called out, "then you have nothing to hide!"

"I have this!" Thalthas growled over his shoulder, not once taking his eyes off of Erik. "May I?" he asked as he gestured toward the cottage; his tone more congenial as he addressed the boy.

Erik stood silently for a moment before finally answering. "Just you – nobody else."

"Agreed," Thalthas said. He glanced at his men. "You two will wait here." The men said nothing as their commander moved past Erik and walked up to the cottage. He hesitated briefly at the door, and then went inside.

Erik turned and looked at the two Riders; both of whom were staring at him apprehensively. He watched, mildly interested, as the two men squirmed in their saddles. They were both fearful of having been left alone with Merlin's apprentice; the stories about what he truly was having now grown to epic proportions since his last visit. Erik could not put his finger on it, but he was almost certain that he had seen one of the two men before.

After some time, Thalthas exited the cottage and walked past Erik without a word, but the look on his face spoke volumes. His men watched curiously as he mounted his horse and turned to leave. Erik felt a pit forming in his stomach as he looked anxiously back and forth from the cottage to Thalthas.

"Well, Commander?" one of the men asked fretfully. "What of the wizard?"

Thalthas turned and stared at Erik before addressing the Rider. "The man whom we were ordered to locate is not in the cottage. It seems that King Lathos has been misled."

"Misled?" the Rider questioned, his voice filled with doubt. "That cannot be. I wish to see for myself!"

Thalthas glared at the Rider, "Be my guest, Verthos. I am sure that you remember the human, and the stories that they tell about him. I can only hope that he has forgotten your rude behavior toward him when he last visited Avalon. As I recall, you were quite eager to engage him in battle when we escorted him and the others to Castle Thoron."

Verthos watched as Thalthas dug his heels into his mount and rode off, back in the direction from which they had come. The other Rider wasted no time in following after their commanding officer. Hearing what sounded like laughter, Verthos turned and faced Erik; horrified to see the human's bright yellow eyes glowing with recognition.

The boy that he had taunted on that first trip to the castle stared keenly at him, his smile filled with razor sharp teeth.

"W-we will find your master!" Verthos said shakily before riding off into the forest, eager to catch up with Thalthas and his comrade.

Erik watched, making sure that the men were well out of sight before running back inside the cottage. The sight of Merlin, Tanna, and his friends sitting around a small table caught him off guard.

"What happened?" he asked excitedly. "I thought we were done for!"

"It seems," Merlin said somewhat distracted, "that we have a friend inside the castle."

"Thalthas?" Erik asked. "But I thought that he was loyal to the king. What changed his mind?"

"He *is* loyal to the king," Tanna said, "it just depends on which king you are referring to."

"Isn't that dangerous?"

"Very much so," Merlin said as his eyes grew dark. "I only hope that what he has agreed to do does not lead to his demise."

*　*　*

Shlogg had not been happy when he had learned that he and the others were being forced to leave the mound. He had felt quite at home there; its labyrinth of lightless tunnels with their smooth white walls reminded him of his own land far to the south of Morgesh Por. Now, he had taken up residence within the lower levels of Castle Thoron, where he maintained control of the dungeons. He had grown accustomed to the cool, dank, and moldy walkways; the cells with their many disillusioned inhabitants — all hope of ever seeing the light of day again long since abandoned — elicited something akin to gratification from deep within him. It was a feeling he looked forward to each and every day.

Now he stood within the throne room, summoned like a common peasant and led through the castle like chattel, where an agitated and clearly rankled Lathos now paced back and forth. A servant had offered Shlogg food and drink, but the troll king had pushed him away angrily.

The light streaming through the windows hurt his eyes and forced him to squint. Shlogg hated the light — always had, always would. The blinding rays from the luminous star were extremely painful to him and his kind, and he despised being exposed to it. With that being said, he despised being at the beck and call of Lathos even more.

Using his hand to block out the irritating sunlight, Shlogg stared icily at the ruler of the tribe of Gorias. Lathos was nothing like his younger brother. Elwyn was an adolescent. A man-child filled with and ruled by a pathetic rage that was fueled by a naïve, petty sibling rivalry. As a ruler he was insecure, and it showed in the way that he behaved and carried himself.

Lathos was different. He was cold, calculating, and cunning. There was a ruthlessness that one could see in his eyes. Lathos craved power, and he would do anything to achieve it. Shlogg knew, better than most, that Lathos would kill anyone who got in his way.

"You called me up here," Shlogg hissed, "to tell me that you wish to dissolve our partnership with the witch? Clearly, it is *you* – not her – who has lost their grip on reality! If she even suspected that we were having this conversation we would be dead but with a blink of her eye!"

"You give Morgan le Fay too much credit...," Lathos scoffed.

"And you give her far too little."

Lathos waved the troll's warning away with a flick of his hand. He sat down at a nearby table; foregoing his throne chair in an attempt at assuring Shlogg that they were indeed equals, and gestured at the chair across from him. Shlogg glanced briefly at the chair before begrudgingly taking the seat offered by Lathos.

"I am convinced," Lathos said with a conspiratorial tone in his voice, "that she has abandoned us already. This entire debacle is solely about what Morgan le Fay wants. None of this is about conquest – it is all about vengeance."

"As I understood it," Shlogg said slowly, "that was all part of the plan. First, she would eliminate the old wizard, and then the children would be taken out of the equation; thus providing us with an unfettered opportunity at taking possession of the Northern Isle..."

"Yes," Lathos agreed. "That *was* the plan. And perhaps, had she upheld her end of the bargain, I would be more inclined to advocate in her defense."

Shlogg eyed Lathos curiously. "I do not understand..."

"She lied to us," Lathos said. "The wizard is not dead. In fact, he is here in Avalon. Very much alive, and about to become even more powerful than ever before!"

"What?!" Shlogg snarled. "T-these are lies! She told us..."

"...that the mage was dead; destroyed by her very hand. None of it is true. As a matter of fact, I have men out looking for Merlin even as we speak." Lathos watched the troll as he digested this latest bit of information. "Why not ask her yourself if you doubt me."

"She has returned?' Shlogg asked. "She is back? Here in Avalon?"

"Were you not informed?" Lathos said casually as he poured himself a glass of wine. "I *am* shocked. I was of the understanding that she kept you apprised on all of her plans and schemes. You *truly* were unaware that she had returned to try and locate the sorcerer?"

"I...I have been...busy," Shlogg said shakily.

"Yes, I am quite sure that you have been," Lathos smirked. "Do not worry, I am quite certain that she plans on filling you in completely on what she is doing in due time."

"You," Shlogg said cautiously, "you truly believe that she has no intention of following through with our agreement?"

"I truly believe that Morgan le Fay wants two things: the Elementals eliminated, and the power of Merlin for herself. We, my dear friend, are merely cannon fodder."

Shlogg's stomach tightened painfully as he thought about the implications of his next decision. If he were to side with Lathos, only to find out later that he had been deceived, Then Morgan's wrath would be great and her punishment unmerciful. If, however, he stayed loyal to the witch, and if what Lathos had told him was indeed the truth, he would be ensuring that he and his people would be Morgan's slaves for all eternity. He glared at the Sidhe king as his wet tongue flicked across one of his eyeballs.

"Tell me," he hissed, "what it is that you want me to do."

8. What Once was Hidden

Zoe watched from the darkened window as Erik, in his demonic form, disappeared into the dense treeline. She knew that he would not go far; that he would conceal himself deep enough within the forest in order to keep watch and prevent anyone else from approaching the cottage and surprising them. She continued to look out the window long after she lost sight of him until the relative stillness of the woods returned; and with a sigh, returned her attention to the conversation at hand.

"I know exactly what you're going to say," Blair stated firmly as she watched Merlin move single-mindedly about the room.

"Hmmm...?" Merlin said absently, glancing back at Blair briefly before returning to his task. "You do, do you? Well, please be a dear and enlighten us all. Tell us what it is that I am about to say."

"You're going to tell me," she said unfazed by his stinging response, "that Thalthas' warning about the trolls changes things. You're going to tell me that it would be crazy to attempt to free Nionia and Gailon from the dungeons with what we now know."

"Um-hmm," Merlin grunted. He busied himself at a bookshelf; pulling several old, and dusty tomes from their places and leafing through them. Growing upset because he could not find what he was looking for, he slammed the books back into place one by one. "Go on," he said without looking at Blair, "surely you have more than that to say. I would think that my rants are a bit more verbose."

"I just wanted to make it clear to you that *nothing* is going to keep me from going after my mother," Blair huffed. "Not you – not anyone!"

"My dear child," he said, finally turning to face her, "I had no intention of trying to keep you from going to free Nionia."

"You weren't?" Eryn asked, shocked. "But aren't you worried about the trolls?"

"I most certainly am, poppet," he said as he began rifling through a set of drawers. "But I am absolutely certain that if our friends are not rescued soon that their fates will be far worse off than they currently are."

"What do you mean?" Angelica asked.

"Once Lathos learns that you all have returned to Avalon," Elwyn answered, "he will undoubtedly use Nionia as bait. He will lay a trap for you, and whether or not it works will mean little to him – in the end, he *will* kill her."

Blair's silvery-white eyes grew wide. "His own mother...but why?!"

"Because he knows that you care about her," Elwyn said sadly. "That, dear sister, is the one advantage that he has over you – over all of us."

"You're describing a monster," she said as she trembled with anger.

"Yes," he agreed. "I am."

Merlin found a wooden crate that had been shoved off into a corner and was digging around inside of it. "Which is why you will need to leave at once. Thalthas is on his way back to report to Lathos, and while he won't admit to finding *me*, he will not be able to hide the fact that he ran into Erik. His own men will divulge that information. And if Lathos learns that Erik is here..."

"Then he'll know that we're here also," Zoe said.

"Precisely," Merlin acknowledged. His search of the crate's interior proved fruitless, and growing frustrated, he pushed the box back into its corner.

"What," a bewildered Tanna asked, "are you looking for?"

"A clue, a map, anything – anything that my other half may have left behind to tell me where he might have hid the staff!" Merlin said angrily.

"So, you do not believe that it is here?" Averyil asked.

"No," Merlin growled. "It will be someplace that would be accessible only by me; and knowing my duplicitous nature, it will be hidden someplace...unique."

"Can't you just summon it?" Eryn asked.

Merlin left the corner and took a seat at the table. "This isn't one of your bloody novels," he said, his features dark. "It doesn't work like that."

"So," Annalise said with a grin as she took a seat beside him, "what you're saying is you've essentially hidden something from yourself, and because you tend to be kind of a jerk sometimes, you don't know how to find it."

"I would not have put it quite so bluntly," Merlin grumbled as he slid a dish back and forth across the top of the table, "but yes."

Tanna walked over to the table staring down at it with a peculiar look in her eye. "What is that?" she asked.

"What?" Merlin scowled at her. "What *are* you going on about?"

Tanna pointed at the table. There, scrawled into the wooden surface was a word: *Nimue*.

Merlin stared at the word as though in a trance, all the while his features brightened and a smile pulled at the corners of his mouth.

"I believe," he said gleefully, "we have found the clue that I have been searching for; and if I am correct, I know exactly where we will find the staff!"

* * *

Thalthas entered Castle Thoron's lower courtyard and urged his mount toward the stables, the two Riders following suit. A stableman approached as Thalthas leaped deftly from atop his horse, and as the man reached for the reins Thalthas waved him away. The servant bowed deeply, grateful for the excuse of not having to deal with the burr-covered animal, before returning to his duties within the stable.

"Verthos," the general called out with a voice tinged with exhaustion as the youthful Rider climbed off of his horse, "tend to the animals, please."

Verthos stared at his commanding officer, confused. "I do not understand. Are we not going to inform the king of our findings?"

"I fully intend on informing the king on all that has transpired," Thalthas sighed. "Now, will you please..."

"But why me?" Verthos demanded as he released his mount's reins and stormed over to Thalthas. "Why should I have to see to the horses? Surely the stablemaster..."

Thalthas grabbed the Rider by the throat and slammed him up against a nearby wall. His face was so close that Verthos could feel the other man's breath against his face.

"You are tending to the horses because I told you to tend to them!" Thalthas barked. "Question another one of my orders and I will – I promise you – put you to the sword! Is that clear?"

"Quite clear, sir!" Verthos choked, the taste of bile strong in the back of his throat.

Thalthas glared at the young soldier for several more seconds before releasing him. Not daring to take his eyes off of his superior, Verthos took the reins of each of the three horses and led them to the stables. Thalthas watched him go into the barn and then gestured for the other Rider to follow him.

The two men proceeded to the throne room in silence. Thalthas' mood was dark and ill-humored, and the lone Rider decided that it would be best if he were to remain silent. Better that then run the risk of becoming his commander's next target. As they neared the large ornate doors, however, Thalthas seemed to calm down. His shoulders, so tense mere moments before, relaxed some; and his face, now clearly visible once he removed his helmet, appeared more fatigued than angry. He stopped just steps from their destination and faced the younger man.

"Your wife was with child," Thalthas said softly, "was she not?"

"Yes sir," the young man said as his chest swelled with pride for the acknowledgment, "she gave birth to our daughter three days ago!"

"May the Gods watch over her," he said, before looking away. "I wonder if I could beg a favor of you, Rider..."

"You have but to ask, sir!"

"I...I was a bit harsh with Verthos back at the stables. It was due to no fault of his own, but to my own frustration in our failure to locate the elderly wizard as requested."

The rider nodded his head. "That is understandable, sir."

Thalthas smiled warmly at the soldier. "I was hoping that you might return to the stables – to offer my apologies to Verthos. I would do it myself, but...," he trailed off as he motioned toward the doorway before them.

"I will relay your explanation, sir. At once!"

"That is a good lad," Thalthas said as he clapped the Rider on the shoulder. "I sincerely appreciate this. Once you have done that, return home and become acquainted with your child."

"Yes, sir. Thank you, sir!"

The Rider saluted before turning back in the direction from which they came. Thalthas watched him warily until he was certain that the soldier was truly on his way back to the stables. He had grown distrustful of others over the last several months – and with good reason. In today's climate, one could never be too sure if one was an actual friend or another of Lathos' spies.

Thalthas took a deep breath and steadied himself for what would most likely be the most important performance of his life. He was a terrible liar, which was probably why he never uttered a single falsehood throughout his life, but this time, things were different. The lives of people that he had grown to care about now hung in the balance and he refused to let them down.

Once again, he ignored the two sentries that stood guard at either side of the doorway and made his way into the throne room. As he entered the chamber, the aroma from the sumptuous meal that had been laid out upon the table before him triggered a gurgling sound from his empty belly. He was acutely aware that he had not eaten since earlier this morning, and some food right now would do wonders for his mood, but he stood silently by and kept his eyes averted from the feast while he waited for his king to receive him.

Lathos stood at a window across the room, his back to Thalthas. He glanced out into the courtyard, the sky slowly darkening and watched as the night fires were being started in the encampments down below. It had become a ritual of his, watching the soldiers as they prepared for the night watch. Knowing that each and every one of the warriors down below would, without question, give their lives to protect him only reinforced in his mind that he was truly the sole heir of all of Avalon, as well as the Northern Isles. He basked in his own glory for a few moments longer before he finally turned his attention to Thalthas.

"My messenger informed me when you approached the front gate. He said that you were alone," Lathos muttered. "Can you explain to me, Commander General, why you have returned to Gorias empty-handed?" Lathos turned away from the window slowly and glared at his officer, immediately despising the military bearing that Thalthas seemed to exude no matter how lowly a task he had been given.

"Earlier we surmised that the wizard would be at the cottage," Thalthas reported as he snapped to attention, "we were wrong."

"We?" Lathos sneered. *"We?* If I recall, it was *you* that assumed that the old man would be at the cottage. If I am incorrect, please tell me so."

Thalthas stood ramrod straight and said nothing in his defense.

"Precisely," Lathos said. "So tell me – did you see *anything* that would have suggested that he had even been there? Anything at all?"

"No, your highness. I saw nothing that would have indicated that the elderly wizard had been there recently."

"So you encountered no one?" Lathos asked sharply.

"Upon approaching the cottage," Thalthas answered, "we did run across one individual. It was the young apprentice – Erik Hedley."

"The human!" Lathos gasped, as an endless number of unforeseen problems for him and his plans ran through his mind due to this latest revelation. "Did...did you speak with him?"

"Yes, my lord," Thalthas said.

After an agonizingly long period of silence, Lathos whined, "And...?!"

"He claimed to be in search of the old mage. I asked him to join us since our objectives were one in the same, but he declined."

"And did you believe him?" Lathos asked.

"No, my lord, I did not."

"But you did not force...encourage...him to return with you. Why not?"

"Since I was not tasked with bringing the apprentice back here, I allowed him to go about his way."

Lathos' face twisted in disgust as he paced about the room. "I assume, then, that he was alone..."

"Was that a question, lord?"

Lathos stared at the warrior from across the room before he stormed over and stuck his finger into the other man's face. "You are trying my patience, Thalthas! Are you attempting to do so deliberately?"

"No, my lord," Thalthas answered.

"Then why," Lathos fumed, "does it feel as if I am having to pull teeth to get answers out of you?"

"My most humble apologies, your highness. It was not my intention to vex you."

"Thalthas," Lathos muttered dangerously, "you are treading upon perilous ground. I suggest that you get out of my sight before I seriously begin to reconsider your position within this court!"

"As you wish, your majesty," Thalthas said as he bowed his head. He took two steps back before turning and leaving Lathos alone in the room.

Lathos' eyes bore into the retreating back of his military commander as he opened and closed his fists angrily. In a rage, he kicked over one of the dining chairs before making his way back to the window. As he stared out into the night sky, the secret door in the rear of the throne room hissed open.

"I presume you heard our conversation," Lathos grunted as a dark figure entered the room from the recessed panel in the wall.

"Yes, my liege. I heard everything."

"Well," Lathos said as he left the window and took a seat upon his throne, "let us hope that *your* report has more to offer in the way of information than the one that I just received!"

"The Commander neglected to inform your majesty that your sister, as well as the other Elementals, were also at the cottage," Verthos said as he bowed gracefully.

Lathos gripped the sides of the throne chair so tightly that his knuckles turned white. "The Elementals are here, as well?!" He cursed Morgan's treachery *and* Thalthas' deception as he tried to collect his thoughts. He pushed himself up and off of the throne, stepping down from the dais on unsteady legs.

"Is...is everything all right, my lord?" Verthos asked anxiously.

"No, you idiot!" Lathos barked. "Everything is *not* all right!" He paused for a moment. "You saw the Elementals – with your own eyes?"

"Yes, my lord," Verthos answered. "I could see them through the window of the cottage as Thalthas was exiting the dwelling."

"And the wizard? Was he there?"

"I did not see the sorcerer; the human would not let anyone enter the cottage but Thalthas."

"I see...," Lathos said.

"Does his majesty require anything more from me?" Verthos asked hopefully.

"Not at the moment," Lathos said absently before waving the Rider off. "You are dismissed."

"It is my intention to always be of service to Gorias' one true King," Verthos fawned as he backed out of the throne room.

Lathos stared at the floor, lost in thought until he heard the large ornate doors bang shut behind him. Walking over to where the chair he had kicked earlier laid, he picked it up and returned it to its place at the dining table. He took a seat and prepared a plate for himself; and as he poured a glass of wine a snarky smile slowly graced his lips.

*   *   *

Tic-Tic lifted his arms up protectively; but though he covered his face with his hands, he was unable to block out the terrifying image of his demise. His screams, barely audible as Malo's foot came crashing down, mingled with the sound of crushed glass as the globe and its contents were ground to bits. The Kelpie moved across the room; hardly taking notice of the fragments of glass and gore on the bottom of his bare foot, as he continued to ransack the book-lined shelves with cold, direful eyes.

"For the life of me," he grumbled as he pushed a set of books onto the floor, "I do not understand why we linger here. It is quite evident that they have come and gone; most likely with the staff, if the report that we received from Lathos is to be believed."

Upon hearing the news concerning Thalthas, the Riders, and their encounter at the cottage, Morgan slipped away from the castle with Malo in tow and proceeded to investigate the lodgings in the Northern Woods herself. Malo had crept silently up to the window in front of Merlin's tiny house and peeked inside. Once he was convinced that the home was vacant, he waved for Morgan to come forward. After assuring herself that the cottage had not been booby-trapped, she and Malo began to tear the place apart in search of anything that could alert them of Merlin's next move.

Morgan now sat across the room with her back to Malo as she perused through several worn books. "I am truly starting to believe," she said under her breath, "that your penchant for stating the obvious is superseded only by your overwhelming necessity to hear yourself speak!"

"What was that you said?" Malo inquired bitterly. "Speak up!"

Morgan sighed as she turned to face him. "I merely said that I put very little faith in the information that we receive from Lathos and his lackeys. It does not matter now – soon, we will be rid of them all." She tossed the book to the floor and, spying a wooden crate in a corner of the room, went over and began rifling through it.

"So why do we waste our time here?" Malo asked again.

"Two reasons," Morgan answered. "First, we must ascertain if they have the staff. If it is indeed in Merlin's possession, well then, that would be unfortunate."

"And second...?"

"Second," she continued, "regardless of whether it is in his possession or not, we must determine where they may have gone."

"But if he has the staff," Malo growled, "what good would that do us?"

"He may have the staff," Morgan said with an exasperated tone, "but he may be too weak to utilize it. If he has not regained his powers the possibility of retrieving it still exists."

"So what is it that you hope to find?"

"Something...anything!" she spat as she dumped the crate's contents onto the floor. It was filled with useless odds and ends; a collection of meaningless objects that had been gathered up and hoarded over the years. Disgusted, she kicked the crate across the floor and made her way over to the table. She plopped down onto the nearest chair and looked over at Malo.

"I am missing something," she hissed. "There must be a reason why they fled!"

"Perhaps," Malo suggested as he wiped his foot on some nearby bed linen, "they feared further confrontation with Lathos' troops."

"Not likely," Morgan argued. "Lathos' army is no match for those girls; let alone their filthy human dog. No – there must be another reason."

Malo took a seat upon the cot across from her. "Is it possible that they could be seeking *you* out?"

"Me?" Morgan grunted.

"You did kill his other half," Malo said with a nod. "If I were Merlin, I would not rest until I had flayed the flesh from your bones and sucked them dry of their marrow."

"You paint such a vivid picture," she said with her mouth twisted in a sneer.

"My apologies," Malo grinned. "It is late and I have not eaten."

"I wish that I had Merlin here now," Morgan said through clenched teeth as she slammed her fists upon the top of the table. "I would rip his heart out and serve it to you garnished with..."

Malo cocked an eye in her direction; alarmed at the bizarre expression on her face. "Morgan? Are you all right?"

A depraved smile perverted the features of her face, as the reflection from the flame of a nearby lantern flickered and danced in her haunted, yet excited eyes. She stared at the table top hungrily before looking up at Malo. "I know where they are going, and more importantly – they do not have the staff!"

"Are you certain?" Malo asked, surprised. He got up from the cot and came over to the table. "Where? Where are they going?"

"You will see soon enough!" she said, giddy as a child on Christmas morning. "I hope that you are hungry..."

"Famished," Malo snarled.

"Excellent," Morgan's voice was cold and malevolent, "because I am about to present you with a banquet the likes of which you have never seen before!"

*   *   *

The voice garbled yet so familiar, tugged at the corners of Nionia's consciousness, in an attempt to pull her from the sleep induced state that she now preferred over that of the waking world. Here, in the recesses of her mind, she could escape the horror of her current situation. Here, she could drown out the screams and the moaning of the tortured souls imprisoned alongside her. Here, she could forget the evil that had consumed her family; the evil that had chased away a daughter, ruined two sons, and decimated her husband. She fought the voice, tried to resist its ever present tug; but in the end, she lost the battle and was pulled, reluctantly, back into the world of the living.

"Mother?" Lathos called out for a fourth time. "Mother – are you awake?"

"What do you want, Lathos?" she whispered. Her voice was hoarse. The cold, damp conditions within the dungeon had sapped her strength – both mentally and physically. Her features were drawn, her body emaciated from lack of food and her hair hung lackluster about her face.

"I merely wished to check up on you," his tone smarmy and insincere. "Is that not the prerogative of a son?"

"I remember my son," Nionia said sadly. "I do not know *what* you are, but you are not my Lathos."

"Mother," he said with a smile, "you cut me to the quick!"

"If only that were true," she said softly. "That, in and of itself, would at least prove that you still had a heart."

"Alron had a heart," Lathos said as he moved away from the door to his mother's cell and approached her small, straw-filled bed, "and look at what that got him. His people mocked him. My heart has been hardened, and because of that I have united the Sidhe!"

"You have done no such thing," she said as she rolled over onto her side to face him. "You have beguiled our people with lies, and they will catch up with you one day."

Although a smile was plastered on his face, he looked upon his mother with scorn. "The Sidhe are weak, as Alron was weak...as *you*, Mother, are weak. One day, you will realize that I speak the truth."

"Please, leave me be." Nionia pleaded as she turned away from her son in disgust.

"As you wish," Lathos said as he turned to leave. He reached for the door latch, and then stopped, as though a thought had abruptly struck him. "I almost forgot to mention," he purred, "your precious little daughter has returned to Avalon."

Nionia's head jerked upward, and a light that had gone out long ago appeared, once again, in her eyes. "Yara?! She is here? Here, in the castle?"

"Calm yourself, Mother!" Lathos said with a grin. "She is nowhere near Castle Thoron; at least I do not believe that she is at any rate."

"She will seek vengeance when she learns what you have done to me – to your brother!" Nionia's eyes began to burn with hatred; it was a look that, for a moment, took Lathos completely by surprise.

"I certainly hope so," he said. "How else am I supposed to lure her here?"

"You would use *me* to ensnare your sister?" she cried. "Why? For what purpose?"

"To rid myself of everything – *everything* – that Alron ever cared about! His time has come and gone. *I* will lead our people into a new age – unencumbered by the anchors that held Alron down!"

"You were heir to the throne," Nionia said as she began to cry, "everything that you stole through deceit would have been yours one day. Why, my son? What did your father ever do to you to deserve such betrayal?"

Lathos left the cell and slammed the door behind him. He looked in at his mother through the heavy bars; his eyes icy and his tone cold.

"What did Alron do to deserve all of this?" Lathos growled. "He lived too long!"

9. The Lady of the Lake

Having no idea where, and if, Lathos had dispatched other Riders, Merlin decided that using a portal to reach their destination would have been an unnecessary risk. The fact that Morgan le Fay had probably returned to Avalon worried him as well. He explained to them that because portals were tears through space, they displaced the fabric of time around them, creating a synchronous vibration that could be followed like a trail of breadcrumbs by someone with the knowledge to do so. Because he did not want to risk their being found, he decided that it would be best to walk to their destination.

Upon leaving the cabin, they had hiked for several hours before they reached a large lake. They were so exhausted after their arrival that they had fallen asleep. All of them, that is, save Erik. He had remained awake, keeping watch throughout the remainder of the night. As daybreak approached, he had awakened them – just as Merlin had requested.

A fragrant breeze nudged the foliage around them as they sat along the edge of the lake and watched the sun begin to rise. The sky, the color of burnt magenta only moments ago, began to give way to morning clouds tinged a bright shade of apricot as the glow from a radiant yellow sun expanded across the water. For just an instant, it appeared as though the beaming orb was rising from out of the lake itself.

"It shan't be long now!" Merlin announced eagerly as he stood up and moved closer to the shoreline. He brushed loose dirt and twigs from his pant legs with an air of preoccupation; all the while, his eyes were fixed firmly upon the center of the vast lake that sat before him.

"So *this* is where we will find the staff?" Annalise asked as she stood and stretched the kinks out of her arms, legs, and back.

"This is *exactly* where we will find it, yes!" Merlin declared.

"So, this is Nimue?" Eryn asked as she took in the scenic landscape.

"Nimue is not a *place*, poppet." Merlin laughed as he looked over at Eryn. "Nimue is a very dear friend of mine!"

"Is she going to meet us here?" Erik asked.

"Meet us here?" Merlin repeated. "Dear Master Hedley – Nimue *lives* here!"

"I haven't seen another cottage since we left yours," Zoe said as she scoured the periphery of the lake. "If she lives nearby, why didn't we spend the evening at her place?"

Merlin picked up a stone and tossed it across the water. He watched the flat projectile as it skipped once, twice, three times along the surface. "Nimue is not the one for entertaining guests."

"Okay," Erik said, "so she's the solitary type. That still doesn't answer the question. Where's her house?"

"I would say right about there," Merlin answered as he pointed toward the middle of the lake. "It's quite an impressive place – or so I've been told."

"Wait...what?" Annalise asked. "She lives out *there*? Are you saying that Nimue is..."

"The Lady of the Lake," Merlin nodded. "Yes, that is exactly what I am saying."

"The same Lady of the Lake that's in the Excalibur story," Eryn asked hesitantly, "*that* Lady of the Lake?"

"One in the same," Merlin affirmed. "Like I said; we've known one another for quite some time."

"The way I remember it from one of my old literature classes from school," Zoe stated, "the two of you had a bit of a thing for one another back in the day. Supposedly, there were some relationship issues..."

"Let's just say that we learned some things about one another over the years and leave it at that; shall we?" Merlin said coolly.

"So why do you think the other Merlin would bring the staff here?" Erik asked as he looked out over the water with renewed interest. "Do you trust her that much?"

"My dear boy," Merlin said, "next to Tanna and you lot, there is no one else that I trust more."

"If she does have it," Zoe asked, "how do we go about getting it back?"

"That's easy – I just have to ask for it," Merlin smiled.

"Just like that?"

"Well," the wizard answered, "not 'just like that.' There *is* an incantation involved." With that, Merlin stepped into the lake; wading forward until the water lapped at his knees. They all watched as the lake's surface became as smooth as glass; and from far beneath its depths, a shimmering burst of light lit up the placid body of water.

"It looks like you got somebody's attention," Eryn whispered excitedly.

"Indeed it does," Merlin said as he felt the air around him crackling with static electricity. He closed his eyes, taking a moment to experience what was happening around him, and then he called out to Nimue.

> *"From waters deep*
>
> *and legends old*
>
> *I have need of what you hold.*
>
> *Return to me what is rightfully mine*
>
> *which was kept secure*
>
> *in your hands divine."*

Merlin stood in the water for a moment longer, before he finally turned and came back to shore. Once more on dry land, he stood alongside the others and stared out at the water.

"I don't understand," Erik said puzzled. "Nothing's happening. Maybe she didn't hear you!"

"Oh," Merlin said softly, "she heard me."

The lake, tranquil just moments earlier, started to foam and churn. The mysterious light that emanated from the water's depths slowly began to coalesce in the lake's center; growing brighter as the water bubbled up as if it were boiling. The hairs on the backs of their necks and arms stood on end as the atmosphere seemed to sizzle, and an enormous geyser erupted abruptly in the very heart of the massive lake.

"Look there," Merlin said excitedly as he pointed out toward the middle of the lake, "there she is!"

Erik and the girls looked out at the lake, their eyes wide with disbelief, as a hand holding Merlin's staff began to rise up from the pool of sloshing water. Bits of vegetation hung wetly from the staff as the appendage that hefted it rose up higher and higher. Awestruck, they watched as the staff was suspended by a hand and an arm visible above the lake's surface; the water around them still once more.

"Isn't she beautiful!" Merlin said, his elation a palpable force that took them all by surprise.

"Where's the rest of her?" Erik asked as he stared at the bizarre, yet strangely compelling, sight before him.

"She's here," Merlin said softly, "she's there…she's all around us! Do you not feel her presence," he asked as he tapped on his chest just above his heart, "here? Do you not hear her song?"

"I *can* feel her," Eryn said slowly, her eyes closed. "She's beautiful!"

"I can feel her, too!" Annalise said.

"I *hear* her!" Zoe whispered, as well. "This is *so* amazing!"

They stood quietly, taking it all in, allowing the essence that was Nimue to overtake and overwhelm their senses. They could taste her kindness. Her generosity was like an intoxicating perfume. They could hear her tenderness; and most of all, they could feel the love that she had for Merlin – it was deep, and ethereal. The sensation was an extremely emotional ride that seemed to have no end.

"Well," Merlin said as he pulled himself reluctantly back to the task at hand, "she will not hold onto the staff forever – someone will have to swim out there and fetch it." He tore his eyes away from Nimue and stared deliberately at Erik.

"Ooh...ooh," Erik said sarcastically, "please let me go and get it, Merlin."

"That's what I admire most about you, my boy," Merlin said as he urged Erik toward the water's edge, "your spunk!"

Hesitantly, Erik walked out into the water and then began to swim out to retrieve the staff from Nimue. Zoe inched her way over to Merlin and gently tugged on the sleeve of his shirt.

"You know," she whispered, "I could have swam out there much faster and gotten the staff for you."

"I'm aware of that," Merlin grinned playfully, "but I do so enjoy that look on his face when I send him off to things like this!"

Erik made his way effortlessly toward the center of the lake; his strokes strong as he moved through the water to get to Nimue and the staff. Nearly there,

he stopped as a thought struck him: Zoe could have swam out, retrieved the staff, and returned with it in the time that it had taken him to get this far. When he heard the laughter from the lake shore behind him he realized fully that he had, once again, allowed Merlin to con him.

Annoyed at his being duped, Erik turned and glared back at his friends, slapping the water irritably. He watched with frustration as Merlin motioned him onward as if to say *'there's nothing that you can do about it now,'* so he grudgingly returned to the task at hand. Erik did an about-face and focused, once again, on the disembodied hand that was sticking out of the water; waiting patiently for someone to come and retrieve the staff. Just as he pushed off again toward his objective, however, he was stopped short. Something, or someone, had grabbed hold of his leg, and before he realized what was happening, he was yanked below the surface.

Merlin and the girls laughed good-naturedly, happy to see that Erik was being a good sport and playing along with them. They watched and waited for him to pop back up, probably somewhere near the staff, but Erik never emerged. The wizard waited a minute more, but when there was still no sign of his apprentice reappearing, his mood turned grave.

"I enjoy a good laugh," Merlin began to grumble, "I really do; but the boy sometimes plays around a bit too much!"

"You did trick him into going out there first," Annalise chided. "Turnabout's fair play!"

"Not at a time like this!" Merlin snapped. "Nimue won't wait much longer. He needs to get to her and..."

Without warning, Merlin was cut off as Erik popped back up out of the water. Gasping loudly, Erik struggled to take air into his lungs as he tried to fight off a large, heavily built man with long sable hair. Bits of weeds and lake muck covered the stranger's face, but the hatred in his eyes was visible even from where they all stood. Erik gagged as his mouth filled with water, and once again he disappeared beneath the surface.

"By the Gods," Merlin cried, "that was a Kelpie!"

*   *   *

The stench of ozone had hardly left the air as they made their way through the dark tunnels underneath Castle Thoron. Blair took the lead position as they made their way to the dungeons. While everyone else eyed the many crosscuts and murky shafts for any trolls that might have been lying in wait, Blair scanned the path ahead; her heightened vision quickly distinguishing the shadows before her as non-threatening outcroppings or rock formations. Having no real track of time, she was not sure

218

how long they had been walking. The tunnels seemed to go on forever, and she was growing more and more anxious the further along that they went.

"How much farther?" she called back to Elwyn irritably.

"We are nearly there!" he whispered harshly. "Now keep your voice down – are you trying to get us captured?!"

Tanna reached out and placed her hand on Blair's shoulder. "We all want to find Nionia," she whispered knowingly, "but we will be no good to her, or the other prisoners if we allow ourselves to be caught!"

"You're right," Blair said softly, regaining her composure. "I'm sorry."

"There is no need to apologize," Tanna smiled, "we understand exactly how you are feeling."

Blair nodded her head and then continued down the tunnel. Once or twice she had touched the walls, pulling her hand away quickly as they made contact with the slick-feeling lichen growing on them. The passageway was damp, the air somewhat chilly, and Blair longed to leave. There was a direful feeling about the place; it smelled of sweat, anxiety, dread, and dismay. Blair knew this scent well, she had experienced it once herself. It was fear – the fear of being locked away and unsure of your fate. She hated the smell; she hated it and the memories that it evoked within her.

Averyil motioned for everyone's attention as she pointed up ahead. "The dungeons," she whispered, "we are here!"

Their approach was hidden by a broad rock shelf. They peered over a ledge and observed a large open area beneath them with cells and cages of various sizes. While some of the cell doors were equipped with what appeared to be small peep holes, there were several that were not. The cages were empty, their purpose a mystery, but what interested them all the most was the lone sentry at the end of the chamber.

"Is anyone else having a déjà vu moment?" Angelica asked as she surveyed the chamber below them.

"If you are implying that this looks like a trap," Elwyn said, "then I must agree with you."

"It is undoubtedly so," Tanna agreed.

"So what's the plan?" Blair asked anxiously. She knew that coming to the dungeons would be difficult – her experience with Elwyn when he was believed to be the Shadow King still caused her to have nightmares; but instead of feeling fearful, she felt only anger. The knowledge that somewhere in this pit, Nionia was being held against her will set her blood to boil. She glared down at the troll who was guarding the cells and wanted to hurt him. She wanted to make him pay – albeit vicariously – for what she had gone through, as well as for what Lathos had done to her mother.

"When last we were here," Averyil commented while scanning the chamber, "there were no less than five guards in this area."

"Well," Tanna whispered, "since it would appear that we are expected, perhaps we should make our presence known."

The guard shifted his weight from one leg to the other, stretched his tired muscles, and then turned and started to make his way across the chamber. As he patrolled the dimly lit corridor he would rake his nails across the doors of the cells as he passed them by; a cruel smile on his lips. As they watched from above, Elwyn's eyes lit up as an idea began to take shape in his head.

"I know just what to do!"

"I'm almost afraid to ask," Angelica sighed, "but what is it?"

"You will see!" Elwyn grinned.

They watched as Elwyn concentrated on the troll as he continued patrolling the hallway. Elwyn extended his hand out slowly, and as he did so a portal opened up in the middle of the floor just steps away from the ghoulish guard. Before he realized what was happening, the troll fell headlong into the black hole. As he disappeared from sight, Elwyn closed the rift; the impish grin still plastered on his face.

"Where did you send him?" Tanna asked warily.

"Who is to say that I sent him *any*where?"

"Are you telling me," Tanna said angrily as she turned and faced Elwyn, "that he is simply lost – floating endlessly through time and space?"

"And if he is?"

"If he is," Blair growled, "then he should consider himself lucky!" With that, the light from her hair and eyes grew in intensity, and she floated up and over the side of the ledge. As she made her way to the floor of the chamber below, the others followed her cue, and leaped over the side of the ledge, as well.

They landed silently as Blair drifted over to the nearest cell door. There was no peephole, so she placed her hands near the large wrought iron hinges. Angelica and the others kept a lookout as Blair's hands became white hot – hot enough that the hinges melted completely away from the huge wooden door. She backed away and nodded at Elwyn, who made his way to the door; knocking it down with one swift, powerful kick.

As they made their way into the cell, Blair was immediately taken aback at the similarities between this room and the one that she had been held in by Shlogg and her brother when they captured her at the mound. The hard, dirt-packed floor was covered in moldy straw. Next to the door, a rat jumped from a bowl; startled by the violent intrusion. They watched quietly as it scurried from the room.

Elwyn glanced into the room and shuddered. "Home, sweet home."

"Not. Even. Funny." Blair warned him as she stared over at him icily.

"It was not meant to be," Elwyn said as he pushed past her. "Lathos had me locked up in this very cell not too long ago…"

"Poor baby," she said as she joined him in the corner of the room where they found a Sidhe sleeping fitfully, curled up on the floor. The man awoke with a start when Elwyn touched him; alarmed at finding himself surrounded by strangers. When he saw that they were not trolls he relaxed just a bit, but only just. It was evident from his condition that he had been down in the dungeons for quite some time – starved, possibly tortured, and left to die. Slowly, they helped him up into a sitting position; placing his back up against the wall for support. Tanna looked him over quickly. She was not pleased with what she saw but was convinced that the man was strong enough to answer some questions.

"My name is Tanna," she said softly, "of the tribe Findias. What is your name?" The man seemed to ignore her at first – his attention locked solely upon Blair. It was only after Tanna gave him a quick shake that he finally answered her.

"I...I too an Findias. M-my name is Melas."

"How long have you been down here?" Elwyn asked.

"Long...enough," he said weakly. He blinked his eyes several times, trying to concentrate on Blair. "You...you *are* real!" he said finally.

"Excuse me?" Blair said as she stared at Melas curiously.

"The...fire goddess," he smiled; several of his teeth had been knocked out of his mouth. "The old man...Gailon, he would...he would tell us tales...tales about you. You...and the others."

"Gailon!" Averyil said excitedly. "You know of Gailon?! Is he here? Is he...is he alive?"

"Alive...?" Melas thought for a moment. "Yes...the old one still lives. At least...he was alive this morning..."

Blair reached out and grabbed Melas by the shoulder; from his reaction, she realized that she had gripped him a bit too tightly. "Sorry," she apologized hastily, "but I need to know – what about Queen Nionia?"

Melas' watery eyes became clearer and more focused. "I am ashamed to admit it, but she is. She should not be down here," he said, his anger rising. "A lady of her stature should *never* have to see a place such as this; let alone be held here as a prisoner!"

"So she *is* here!" Blair cried out excitedly. She was torn; happy to have found Nionia, but distressed at the knowledge that she had been locked away in a place like this for so long.

"Yes," Melas said, "Gailon...your queen, they are here; as well as many others."

"Not for much longer," Tanna said as she made her way back toward the cell door. She poked her head out and looked around before motioning to the rest of them. "We need to free the other prisoners and get out of here. If we *have* walked into a trap I fear that it won't be long before Shlogg orders it sprung!"

* * *

"What's he doing out there?" Eryn asked frantically as she stared out at the lake. "Why doesn't Erik transform?!"

"He's unable to," Merlin said. The shame that he felt because of his inability to help his friend could be heard in his voice. "The Kelpie is a creature of dark magic. As long as it maintains its grip on Erik he will be unable to transform!"

Zoe quickly pushed past the wizard and dove into the water. Within seconds she was in the spot where they had last seen Erik and the Kelpie. She plunged under the surface; her eyes darting in every direction until she found them. She watched, horrified, as Erik wrestled with the monster; all the while, he was being pulled deeper – down to the very bottom of the lake.

Zoe soared through the water, reaching them so quickly that the force of the impact nearly propelled them all across the lake. As she came up behind the Kelpie she wrapped her arms around the creature's throat. The beast tensed up, startled by the unexpected attack, but continued to grapple with Erik. As the boy struggled, the Kelpie tried to shake itself free from Zoe's grasp. She jerked back fiercely with enough force to snap a large tree branch in two, but the behemoth only fought harder.

Erik's eyelids began to flicker as his pupils rolled; a steady stream of bubbles that escaped from his lips became a mere dribble as he slowly slipped into unconsciousness. Terrified for him, Zoe raked her fingers furiously across the Kelpie's eyes. She could almost hear the fiend's screams of pain as though they were standing on dry land; and wracked with pain, Malo released his prey. Erik's limp form drifted slowly away as the monster sought to protect itself.

Zoe released the Kelpie and went after Erik. She caught him by the arm, and pulling him close to her, she raced toward the surface. She moved speedily through the water, even with Erik's added weight, but she could sense that the Kelpie was not far behind them. She could feel the monster's presence – not only in the water but within her mind as well.

"*I* will *kill you*," Malo's voice wailed in her thoughts. "*Neither you or the man-demon, stand a chance against me! This may be* your *element, but it is mine, also. Give up, and I will make your deaths quick and painless!*"

No longer able to see Erik or her sister, Annalise stood on the lake shore desperately trying to make contact with her. The images that came back to her when she attempted her mind link were frightening. The mental pictures were savage, bloodthirsty, and gruesome. It was as though someone else's thoughts were overriding Zoe's; almost as if Annalise was being warned not to interfere unless she wanted to share in her sibling's fate.

"Nimue!" Merlin's cries broke Annalise's telepathic link. "If she returns to the lake the staff will be lost forever!"

Annalise looked out at the middle of the lake and saw that, indeed, the hand that was holding the staff was slowly sinking back into the water. Without a second thought, she shot across the lake, flying several feet above the water; her hand outstretched to retrieve Merlin's staff. Just as Nimue's hand disappeared beneath the surface, Annalise snatched up the magical artifact; and as the Lady of the Lake receded into the water, the glow that had illuminated the lake just moments before was extinguished, as well.

With the staff in her possession, Annalise scoured the lake in search of a sign of her sister or Erik. She did not have to wait long; Zoe shot up from the water – her eyes wide and filled with fear. She looked up and saw Annalise, waving at her anxiously.

"Over here!" she yelled. "Help me...get Erik out of here!" She held him close as he coughed up water and bile.

Annalise flew to them hurriedly, her hand extended out to take hold of Erik's. She grasped his wrist firmly and lifted him out of the water, but with the staff in her other hand, she was unable to pull Zoe out also. She grew frantic as a pair of glowing eyes made their way toward Zoe from the lake's dark depths.

"Give me the staff!" Eryn yelled as she flew over and came alongside Annalise. "Quickly – give me the staff so you can help Zoe!"

Annalise nodded to her friend thankfully and tossed the staff over to Eryn. She caught the artifact and smiled before turning and making her way hastily back to shore. No longer concerned about Merlin's relic, Annalise turned her attention back to Zoe. She reached for her sister's hand and was about to pull her from the water when the Kelpie surged from its depths. Caught off guard, Annalisescreamed as Malo pushed Zoe back under the water, using her as a brace to propel himself upward, in an attempt at getting to Annalise and Erik. She launched herself higher into the air as Malo came crashing back down and disappeared into the lake once again.

"Zoe!" Annalise cried out as the water's surface became as smooth as glass once more. In shock, she hovered there, staring down at the lake in disbelief.

"Let me go," Erik croaked, his voice hoarse and scratchy from vomiting.

Stunned to find Erik conscious, let alone speaking, Annalise locked eyes with him. "W-what?" she sputtered, confused.

"Let. Me. Go!" he growled more forcefully. His eyes burned hot yellow like the sun. He did not have to repeat his request a third time; aware of his intentions Annalise complied, and Erik, too, disappeared into the lake's murky expanse.

Desperately, she tried to peer into the inky black water for any sign of what could be going on underneath the lake's surface; but all she got for her efforts was her own reflection which bobbed and weaved atop the rippling water. Frantic for answers, and afraid for her sister, Annalise was about to reach out to Zoe telepathically one more time, but she hesitated when the water beneath her began to froth and bubble violently.

Annalise inhaled sharply as the spot where she had watched Erik go under became blood-red and foamy. Her lower lip began to tremble as she imagined the worst. Silently, she held her hand out toward the water hoping against hope, when the lake erupted fiercely all around her. She shielded her face with her hands, attempting to block out the blinding cascade of water. As the downrush cleared, she was astonished at finding Zoe safe and unharmed – nestled protectively within the arms of Erik's demonic conformation.

"You're safe!" she cried as tears of joy commingled with the lake's water that dripped from her face. "What happened down there?"

"Trust me," Zoe said as she glanced at Erik uneasily, "you don't want to know!"

"But what about the Kelpie?" Annalise asked anxiously. "Will it be coming back?"

"We have no reason to fear the Kelpie any longer," Erik growled as his powerful wings flapped behind him. "What is most important right now is the location of the staff. Were you able to recover it?"

"No worries," Annalise said as she took note of the troubled look in Zoe's eyes as she stared at Erik, "I gave it to Eryn. She took it back to shore to give to Merlin."

"Then might I suggest that we make our way back to shore as well," Erik said as he turned, his massive wings carrying he and Zoe back to the other side of the lake. Annalise took one last look at the bloody water below her, and as a shiver crawled down her spine, she too flew off in the direction of the lakeside where Merlin and Eryn were waiting.

Eryn and Merlin watched as Annalise flew off to retrieve the staff before Nimue's hand slipped beneath the water with the relic forever. An opaque mist began to blanket the area about the lake, blotting Annalise and the

232

others from view. Eryn, fretting for her friends, took a step toward the lake, and then looked over at Merlin worriedly.

"What's going on?" she asked anxiously. "This mist — is this normal? We can't see a thing!"

"Things like this happen all the time around large bodies of water," Merlin said as he tried to peer through the dense fog, "I wouldn't worry about it."

"So," Eryn said skeptically, "you're not worried about them out there?"

Merlin continued to stare out at the lake without saying a word. After several moments of silence, he cut his eyes over at Eryn, noticing her hands on her hips, and then turned to face her. "Of course I'm worried about them," Merlin said.

He took several steps away from the lake before he dropped down onto the ground. As he sat there, staring once again at the lake, Eryn noticed that the haughtiness that he normally exhibited seemed to have vanished just as quickly as the strange mist that had enveloped them had appeared.

"You were right, you know, back at Tanna's," Merlin said quietly as he glanced at Eryn, "I've done nothing but put you all in danger since the moment I made myself known to you."

"I didn't say that exactly," Eryn said sheepishly as she took a seat beside the wizard. "I was just trying to get my point across."

"You're mother didn't seem to have any problem with that."

"My mom has got a way with words," Eryn grinned

"She's also got a pretty mean right hook," Merlin said as he rubbed his chin.

"I'm sorry about that," Eryn apologized, "but you have to realize that she was really scared for me. She was pretty angry, too, but mostly she was scared."

"I understand completely," Merlin said. "You have no need to apologize for her, or for any of the other parents, for that matter. What I did to them was terribly wrong. I should have been upfront with all of them from the very beginning. With the task that I was placing upon them, they had every right to know what they were getting involved in."

"You'll get no argument from me," Eryn said as she looked out at the lake.

"Now my friend is out there having to deal with a savage Kelpie – all because of me!"

"Do you think Zoe and Annalise will be able to help him?

"It's hard to say," Merlin said as he wrung his hands. "For all I know, he is out there fighting for his life and here I sit, completely helpless."

"Not completely helpless," Eryn said. "I'm here."

"And for that I thank you," Merlin said. "I know what coming back here has cost you."

"I will admit that I did not want to come back here," Eryn said as she locked eyes with him, "this place, the creatures and people who live here, it's not me. I may have been born here, but outside of that I don't really want anything to do with Avalon." Eryn stood up and looked down at Merlin. "I am not Raina of the tribe of Murias; I'm just plain old Eryn Friar of Traverse City, Michigan. I'm happy with that, believe it or not. I was blessed with abilities, and I know that certain obligations come with powers like the ones that I possess, but I will not be *defined* by those abilities. Do you understand?"

"More so than you know, Poppet!" Merlin said with a smile as he glanced up at Eryn. He began to stand up, and as he did he noticed a peculiar look in her eyes. "What is the matter, child?" he asked. "You look as if you have seen a ghost."

Eryn stared fixedly at the tree line behind them, her face a mask of fearful apprehension. "W-what are those...those *things*?!"

Merlin stared at her curiously before he turned to look at what the girl was gesturing at. His eyes grew wide as he watched hundreds – no, thousands – of tiny creatures climbing out from the woods behind them. They were approximately eight inches tall, with long pointy ears and horns atop of their heads. Their skin was a deep green, as green as the leaves in the trees that were all about them; they had long tails, eyes that glowed a yellow-orange, and they walked upon cloven-hooved feet.

The strange creatures approached the pair menacingly. Some of them carried large sticks that they beat against the ground over and over again in an attempt to frighten Merlin and Eryn, while others clicked their long claws and sharp teeth in anticipation for a confrontation. Slowly, yet steadily, the little monstrosities made their way forward, as Merlin and Eryn backed up to the water's edge.

"I think it's time," Merlin whispered harshly, " for you to use those abilities that you didn't want to be defined by!"

As the three of them landed upon the shore, they were shocked to find no one waiting there for them. Erik placed Zoe gently on the ground and walked ahead of his friends, sniffing the air as he went. He pulled his wings in closely against his back as he peered into the tree line; his lips curled back from his teeth as he registered the sensory signals around him.

"Something is wrong," he muttered.

"Ya think...," Zoe said sarcastically.

"What I mean," he said as he eyed her intensely, "is that someone or some*thing* has been here besides Merlin and Eryn. I am also detecting signs of a struggle."

"Merlin!" Annalise yelled, cupping her hands around her mouth. "Eryn!"

"Over here...!" Merlin called from behind a thick growth of bushes.

Erik vaulted over the thicket and was by his mentor's side in an instant. Annalise and Zoe made their way gingerly through the bushes. Once clear of the dense vegetation, they ran over and joined Erik and their friends. They were stunned to see Eryn lying in Merlin's arms, her face and arms covered in cuts and scratches. Her eyelids were beginning to flutter, as though she were just waking up from a nap.

"What happened?" Zoe asked nervously as she took in Eryn's present state. "Is she okay?"

"I believe so," Merlin said as he helped Eryn sit up. "We were attacked by imps – thousands of them! The vile little creatures came out of the woodwork and commenced biting, scratching, and clawing at us from every direction. Eryn was able to summon up a wind to scatter most of them across the four realms, but not before one of the little buggers struck her on the back of the head with a rock!"

"Then I presume that it was one of these *imps* that must have stolen the staff from you?" Erik asked, his voice grave as he noted the absence of the relic.

"The staff – stolen?" Merlin said, confused. "What are you talking about? Annalise has the staff; I watched her go to retrieve it from Nimue!"

"I took it from her," Annalise answered, "but then I gave it to Eryn!"

Merlin's eyes, filled with dread, flashed from Erik to Annalise. "Child – what *are* you playing at?"

"The Kelpie was coming after Erik and Zoe, and I couldn't pull them both from the lake," Annalise explained, "because I was holding the staff. That's when Eryn flew over and...," her voice dropped off when the realization of what had truly occurred struck her.

"I...I c-can't f-fly...," Eryn mumbled shakily.

"Eryn never left my side," Merlin insisted. "She has been here, *with me*, from the moment that *you* left to get the staff!"

"Then," Annalise stuttered, "then who did I give the staff to?" She was afraid that she already knew the answer to her question.

"I think we all know who took it," Merlin said fearfully. He looked at each of them in turn. "If we don't get that staff back from Morgan, and soon, then all of Avalon is doomed!"

10. The Dungeons of Thoron

Blair stood up and joined Angelica at the doorway, as Elwyn and Averyil took hold of Melas' arms in order to assist him to his feet. The Sidhe shook them both away proudly and climbed up from the floor.

"I do not mean to be rude, my lady," he said to Averyil before turning to Elwyn. "Nor do I mean you any disrespect, my prince, but I am Melas, son of Ne'lonn of the tribe Findias – I will walk under my *own* power!" He stumbled a bit at first but eventually made it to the doorway with the others.

Still seemingly undetected by any other troll guards, they quickly, and quietly, returned to the outer chamber. There were approximately eleven more cell doors left; cells that, according to Melas, could contain anywhere up to four prisoners each. They did not have the time, or the luxury to investigate each cell one at a time in order to locate Gailon; Schlogg and his men could be on them at any moment and they preferred to complete this mission without a confrontation. Tanna made her way over to her granddaughter and took her gently by the arm.

"We are going to need you to open these doors, Angelica." she said as she led the girl to the center of the room.

Angelica glanced up at the rocky ceiling high above them. "It'll be tricky – if I can shift the walls away from the floor and door jambs several inches without disturbing everything sitting on top of us too much, it should be enough to free the cell doors…"

"Mere child's play for one such as yourself," Elwyn said confidently. "What could possibly go wrong?"

"Oh, I don't know," Angelica answered. "I mean there is an entire *castle* filled with hundreds of people right above us!"

"You will do just fine," Tanna said, pushing Elwyn back and out of the way. "Everyone move away and give her some room, we're running out of time!" Tanna nodded at Angelica. "You can do this – you just have to concentrate."

"Yes, Gran," Angelica replied as they gave her a wide berth. She closed her eyes and focused her mind on the ground directly beneath her feet. Within moments she felt the familiar tingle that emanated from her solar plexus, followed quickly by an inner peace that seemed to envelop her entire body. She opened her eyes, her face set, and knelt down on one knee. Placing a hand upon the ground, Angelica smiled as she felt the earth begin to move.

Seismic fissures shot away from where she knelt, racing outward toward each of the cell doors. The cracks in the stone crust inched their way up the walls alongside each of the doors, coming to a stop precariously close to the chamber's ceiling. With a final look of determination, she pushed her hand down into the floor; sending a concussion wave along each fissure. Now free of the hinges that held them in place, one by one the doors fell free from their jambs; and as she returned slowly to her feet they came crashing down with a resounding thud – the noise bouncing back and forth throughout the chamber.

A clamor rang out above them, as the harsh sound of rage, weaponry, and the soles of bare feet slapping upon the stone floors made their way down into the chamber. The trap had been sprung, and now Shlogg's men were moving toward them. Blair and the others made their way to each of the cells; extricating each of the captives from their prisons, and gathered them all up in the center of the chamber. It was Tanna who arrived with an ill-treated, yet defiant Gailon in her arms.

"Grandfather!" Averyil cried as she rushed over to him. The two embraced, but only briefly before he pulled himself away.

"Zoe," he asked anxiously, "Annalise...your sisters, are they safe?!"

"We certainly hope so," Tanna answered quickly. "They are on a separate mission of grave import with Merlin."

"Merlin?" Gailon said, confused. "But I...I thought that the wizard was dead..."

"It's a long story," Blair said dismissively as she shoved her way toward Gailon. "Where's Nionia? She wasn't in any of the other cells!"

"The Queen...?" Gailon answered vacantly. "She is no longer here..."

"What do you mean?" Blair demanded. "Melas told us that she was alive!"

"And so she is," Gailon reassured her, "but Shlogg and his men came and took her away long before you showed up."

"The same men," Tanna warned, "that are on their way here now!"

"Took her where?" Blair asked eagerly. "Please, Gailon! Where did he take her?"

"At the end of this chamber," Gailon said, "there are a set of stairs. They will take you up to the next level. I am told that there is a vast storeroom..."

"Indeed there is," Elwyn chimed in. "It holds one of the castle's largest munitions caches."

"Yes," Gailon confirmed. "That is where he took her."

"Why would he take her there?" Angelica asked.

"Because he knows that it is the one place that I wouldn't dare use my abilities," Blair grumbled. "He set this trap for me. Elwyn," she said as she looked at her brother, "get everyone out of here. Can you lead the way?"

"Of course I can...," he began, but Blair was gone before he could finish.

*   *   *

The barrage of ice-cold water pulled Thalthas back from a dark pool of unconsciousness. Wracked with pain, his entire body trembled furiously;it was not because of the shock from the sudden ice bath, but from the extreme torture that he was being put through. His left eye swollen shut, he glared at the troll who had thrown the freezing water over him.

After his meeting with Lathos, Thalthas had left the throne room acutely aware that the young king had endured the Commander General's insolent behavior for the very last time. So he was not surprised the next day when, having made it to the commissary for the morning meal, a squad of trolls marched up to his table brandishing their weapons. He was also not surprised when Verthos made his way forward and announced that Thalthas was under arrest for espionage by order of the King. One of the trolls' snatched him from his seat, where they then proceeded to drag Thalthas from the commissary like a common criminal to the courtyard where Laths was waiting. Without the slightest acknowledgment to his rank or status, the order was given to extract information from him.

"King Lathos," the scaly-skinned tormentor hissed, "he is awake..."

"Ask him again," Lathos commanded from across the courtyard.

Thalthas had been suspended by his wrists between two large poles; the tips of his toes barely touching the ground. Stripped of his shirt, he had been whipped until his flesh bled. Open wounds crisscrossed his chest, shoulders, and back. The areas of his body that had not been torn open by the lash were covered in dark bruises and discolored markings of various shapes and sizes. The troll walked up to Thalthas and grabbed a handful of hair, yanking his head up violently.

"Where are the Elementals?" the troll grunted.

Thalthas stared at the creature with his one good eye but remained silent. His chest heaved painfully each time that he drew a breath; the very effort setting his lungs on fire. The troll nodded his head, and grinning, struck Thalthas in the jaw with his fist. Blood flew from the warrior's mouth as the strike ripped open his lower lip. Dazed, Thalthas had barely begun to register the pain from this latest assault when the troll grabbed him by the hair again.

"Where is Merlin?!" the brute roared as he drew his fist back to throw another punch.

"Wait!" Lathos called out as he approached the two men. He waved the troll away as he stepped up and looked at Thalthas appraisingly. Lathos' features were cold and unfeeling as he peered into Thalthas' eye. "Why are you doing this? Why will you not answer my questions?"

"I...I have...I have no answers for you...," Thalthas said shakily.

"Where is your loyalty to your king?" Verthos demanded as he came up from behind Lathos.

"I will always be King Alron's most loyal of subjects!" Thalthas said, the strength in his voice returning as he eyed the traitorous young Rider.

"I," Lathos roared, "am your king! That is why you are in the predicament that you currently find yourself – you are blind to reality. You refuse to accept what is. *I* am King! Alron is dead!"

Lathos turned and walked away, gesturing to the troll to continue his work. The troll bent over and picked up a small iron mace. It was a nasty looking implement, capped with an iron ball that was studded with dozens of small, blunted spikes.

The troll's eyes burned with anger as he gripped the mace tightly in his hand; his anger stoked by Thalthas' continued refusal to answer his questions. He despised the Sidhe; their holier-than-thou attitude, their unwavering

248

sense of entitlement. The longer Thalthas withheld the information that Lathos wanted, the longer the troll had to remain exposed to the accursed daylight.

He drew the mace back, about to strike Thalthas with it, when he was stopped short by a strange smell. All activity in the courtyard ceased as a portal began to yawn open within their midsts. Soldiers, the vast majority of them ordered to the courtyard to witness Thalthas' degradation, backed away cautiously as the rift grew in size and shape. Lathos scowled as he stared angrily into the portal; not the least bit surprised when Morgan le Fay stepped out of it.

"My goodness," she cooed as she glanced over at Thalthas. She took in the scene around her for a moment before she turned and faced Lathos. "Someone is throwing a party and they failed to invite me! Should I be offended?"

*   *   *

Blair was through the chamber, up the stairs, and past Shlogg's sentries within seconds. At the far end of the corridor was a large door; iron-forged, no doubt, in order to keep beings such as herself from entering. Blair stared at

249

the deadly obstacle for a moment as her entire body became white hot. Her clothing, now completely woven from dragon scales, took on an eerie glow as she slowly approached the door. The heat from her body grew in intensity until, finally, she melted her way through the door.

"Shlogg," she called out disdainfully as her core temperature returned to normal, "I know that you're in here!" Blair made her way into the storeroom. "Where's my mother, you wimp?!"

"This way!" the troll king hissed from out of the shadows.

Blair moved forward stealthily between row after row of boxed explosives, barrels of gunpowder, and other assorted containers full of munitions. She was about to double back; afraid that he was moving from spot to spot, taunting her when she found him – a brutal smile on his face.

Shlogg stood there, arrogantly, surrounded by dozens of barrels of explosives. In his hand was a cruel-looking battle axe; the wooden handle wrapped in leather, and the strap at the end secured to his wrist. Kneeling on the ground in front of him were Nionia and another one of the prisoners. Nionia's mouth had been secured with a gag while, oddly enough, the man beside her had a sack pulled down over his head. Nionia's eyes grew fearful as she watched her daughter approach them.

"Hostages, Shlogg...really?" Blair said, her voice dripping with contempt. "You don't have the guts to face me one on one?"

"My dear child," Shlogg hissed, "you are under the misconception that this was meant to be a fair fight. Sadly, you are mistaken. You should know by now that nothing in life is fair – and if you were *not* aware of that fact, well, it is high time that you learned!"

Blair looked over at Nionia. Her features softened when she saw the despair in her mother's eyes. She took a step toward the queen but was quickly admonished by Shlogg.

"Careful, Princess..." the troll king growled. He hefted the battle axe for emphasis. "You do not want to do something that you may come to regret."

"All I want to do is make sure that Nionia is okay!"

"Oh," Shlogg grinned, "she is quite all right – they are both all right, for that matter."

"Who *is* that?" Blair asked, pointing to the man kneeling beside Nionia. "Why do you feel the need to pull strangers into your twisted game?"

"He is insurance," Shlogg answered. "They are *both* insurance."

"This is insane!" Blair said. "I get it – my mother is bait. That's the oldest trick in the book, but you didn't have to endanger anyone else just to get me here!"

"Really?" Shlogg replied. "Are you saying that you would not have come had you known that...," Shlogg pulled the bag from the prisoner's head with a flourish, "...I held King Alron prisoner as well?"

Blair stepped backward; stunned at the sight of her father kneeling before her. He was now a shadow of his former self. His hair was matted and caked with dirt and gore, his beard had grown unkempt, and his face was drawn. His nose had been broken at some point, and he had lost a tremendous amount of weight. He was shirtless, so she could plainly see the scars that covered his upper body. It was obvious that his captors had tried to break his spirit, but the fire that gleamed in his defiant eyes revealed that they had been unsuccessful.

"I'm here now," Blair murmured. Her voice trembled with rage as she pulled her eyes away from her parents and glared at Shlogg. "You got what you wanted – you can let them go!"

Shlogg's raspy laugh echoed throughout the room. "Oh no, princess!" he hissed. "No one is going anywhere. You see, getting you here was just a part of the plan. There are still two more tasks that need my attention. The first is to rid the world of *your* miserable existence. The second is to remove the crown of Gorias from the head of your worthless brother. Once I have done that, I will make sure that the former rulers here meet a fitting end!"

"Lathos might have something to say about your killing off his family members," Blair said.

"Silly girl," Shlogg chuckled, "it was Lathos who ordered your executions!"

"So Lathos told you to treat my mother this way?" Blair seethed. "Has he been aware of Alron's imprisonment all of this time?"

"It was always Lathos' intention to use your mother as bait," Shlogg gloated, "and as for Alron – the less that Lathos knows , the better off he is. If your brother behaves himself, then he need not ever know that Alron survived the massacre at the mound. However, if he places so much as a toe out of line; well, let us say that the consequences would be dire."

"What about Morgan?" Blair asked, stalling for time. "She won't be too happy once she's learned that you and Lathos cheated her out of her revenge."

"Morgan's time has come and gone," Shlogg answered confidently. "After I have rid the realm of you and your insipid friends, *her* head will be next up on the chopping block. The Trolls will be the true rulers of Avalon – and *I* will be its King!"

"Well I've got some bad news," Blair muttered harshly as her hair grew hot, her eyes glowed fiercely, and the heat from her body warmed the room, "none of it is going to happen!"

"Such brave talk for someone surrounded by all of these explosives. Look around you," Shlogg snarled, "one errant spark and we all die!"

"See my face," Blair snapped, "that's me not caring!" She launched herself at Shlogg, hitting him squarely in the chest with all of her might; the impact sending the troll king flying across the room and slamming him against the wall. Blair raced over to her parents and helped Alron, and then Nionia, to their feet.

"Can you two make it to the stairs?" she asked Alron quickly.

"Yes," Alron answered. "Please, come with us!"

"I've got something to do first," Blair said as she ushered them in the direction of the door. "Now please, go!"

As her parents fled the room, Blair turned and faced Shlogg. The troll king pulled himself from the floor, his expression cold and filled with hate. He gripped the battle axe with both hands and came at her.

"That," he growled, "was a mistake. All you have done is sealed their fate!" He swung the axe, the weapon's cold blade slicing through the air, but its intended target was gone.

"Is that all that you've got?" Blair taunted as she moved out of the blade's path. "I've seen little boys swing baseball bats harder than that!"

Shlogg brought the axe down – aiming for her skull – but once again she dodged the blow. He charged at her, hoping to throw her off her balance, but received a foot in his gut for his efforts. The air shot out of his lungs, and he lost his grip on his weapon. The battle axe fell to the floor, and as he scrambled to retrieve it he failed to notice that Blair was moving about the room, igniting the boxes, barrels, and containers as she went.

"You little brat!" he growled as he moved toward her. "I *will* get you; but believe me, you will not be allowed to expire before I get my hands on your parents!"

"You're not going to harm my parents, or anyone else, anymore!" Blair said angrily.

"I will do more than harm them," Shlogg sneered as he hefted the axe, "I will make them suffer! Tell me, do you know what death looks like?"

In the blink of an eye, Blair was on the troll. She slammed into him so forcefully that he dropped his weapon and fell to the floor. He tried to get up, but the girl pummeled him with more punches than he could count. Enraged, she placed a hand around Shlogg's throat and lifted him up off of the ground. "You tell me," she asked coldly, "is *this* what death looks like?"

Her body temperature rising, Shlogg could feel the skin on his neck beginning to singe. The smell of his burning flesh filled the room as he slowly began to realize that she had ignited the munitions.

"You fool," he gurgled. "The explosives! You will set them off! Your parents could not have made it out in time – we will all die!"

"You were wrong earlier," Blair squeezed his neck even tighter as flames began licking their way up the sides of the boxes and containers, "when you said no one was going anywhere. The only person not leaving this room is you!"

Shlogg's fear-filled screams were drowned out as the barrel nearest him exploded; the resulting cascade, like falling dominos, rocked the entire castle. Mere seconds before the blast tore his body to bits, he caught a fleeting glimpse of Blair – Nionia and Alron in her arms as they sped away from the inferno – and he cursed the day that he had first laid eyes upon her.

11. The King is Dead, Long Live the King!

Lathos ignored Morgan's attempt at levity and signaled to the troll to continue with his work. While Thalthas' grunts of pain echoed throughout the courtyard, Lathos took note of the fact that Morgan now possessed what appeared to be Merlin's staff. The witch followed his gaze, smiling triumphantly.

"Are you not the least bit curious?" she asked as she made her way toward Lathos, brandishing her trophy with pride.

"About the staff?" he inquired gruffly. "I suppose I have to – given your propensity to keep things to yourself."

"Why, whatever do you mean?"

"I assume," Lathos said bitterly, "that you now hold the relic; which can only mean that you found where he was hiding it. How marvelous for you. But you neglected to inform me at our earlier meeting that my sister and her friends had returned to Avalon to aid the old wizard. Did you not think that that would be information that I should have been privy to?"

"Perhaps," Morgan said, her tone aloof. "But truth be told, had you known, what could you have possibly done about it?"

"Watch your tongue, witch!" Verthos growled as he stepped in between Morgan and Lathos.

"And who," she said with a dangerous look in her eye, "might you be?"

"I am Verthos, First Rider elite of the L'Norr, and Commander General of the King's army!"

"Is that so?" Morgan grinned. "Then I would be careful if I were you, little boy," she said as she gestured over her shoulder at the abuse being administered to Thalthas. "I hear that position comes with some very nasty consequences when you misbehave!"

"Enough!" Lathos commanded as he pushed himself up and out of his chair. "You had no right keeping that information from Shlogg and I! Had we known that the Elementals were here sooner we could have made plans..."

"Yes, the two of you *are* good at that sort of thing," Morgan interrupted, "making plans."

"I have absolutely no idea what you are talking about!" Lathos said, caught short by her comment. There was something different about the sorceress. She had an air of arrogance about her; a sense of her own superiority that was more so than usual. Her behavior made him leery — so much so that he had to fight back the urge to turn and run for his life.

"Come now," she said sweetly, "let us not play games with one another. You know exactly what I am talking about! Do not forget, I have spies within the castle, as well. So," she said as she looked around the courtyard, "where *is* your bug-eyed co-conspirator?"

"You are speaking nonsense," Lathos said nervously as he began to turn away.

"Do you truly wish to go down this road, Lathos?" Morgan asked pointedly. "Very well; perhaps it *is* time that I remind you of *who* is actually in charge here."

Morgan took the staff and waved it in the direction of some of the soldiers who were standing in the courtyard. Before Lathos could say a word in protest, fifty of his men fell to the ground. Verthos ran over to them and attempted to administer aid to one of the men. After several seconds he looked over at Lathos; his eyes wide with fear.

"He...they are dead, your majesty!" he said aghast. "They are *all* dead!"

The troll, having witnessed Morgan's display, dropped the mace and ran off in the direction of the castle. The battered Sidhe warrior hung limply from his bound wrists; his agonized wheezing the only sound within the stunned courtyard. The remaining soldiers, alarmed at the fate of their comrades, looked to their king for succor.

"W-what have you done?" Lathos gasped as he stared at Morgan incredulously.

"What have I done?" she echoed. "I was attempting to make a point. Have I succeeded?"

"Yes," Lathos answered quietly as he stared out at the men lying dead before him.

"I am not quite sure that I heard you."

"Yes!" Lathos said loudly. "Yes, you...you have made your point."

"Excellent!" Morgan giggled as she moved past Lathos and took his seat. "Now, I will ask you once more: where is Shlogg?"

"I sent him to the dungeons," Lathos said in a daze as he stared at the dead men lying in the courtyard, "to lie in wait for my sister."

"That does make sense," Morgan acknowledged. "The sentimental twit *will* come for her mother at some point without a doubt. Shlogg and his men should be enough to handle the likes of her."

"I am pleased that you approve," Lathos said sarcastically, "but are you forgetting that there are *five* of them?"

"I have not forgotten," Morgan said, smiling. "By now, we should be down to only two of the insufferable little brats – all thanks to my cunning and an extremely hungry Kelpie! Besides," Morgan said mischievously, "if I were you, I would be more concerned about Alron's likely escape than your infantile sister and her friends. Who knows what kind of damage *he* could cause if he were to leave the dungeons!"

"What are you talking about?" Lathos asked, somewhat disturbed. "Alron is dead..."

"Is he?" Morgan inquired candidly. "Are you quite certain? As the story was relayed to me, Alron survived the battle at the mound. Shlogg brought him here secretly; holding him in the dungeons as a safeguard – just in case you should ever turn on him. You never can trust a troll, you know."

Lathos' gut began to tighten as the implications of Morgan's news struck home. Sweat beaded his forehead as he realized that everything he had built with the sorceress was beginning to crumble all around him. He opened his mouth to plead his case, hoping for forgiveness and hoping to throw Shlogg to the wolves; but before one syllable could pass his lips a tremendous underground explosion rocked the castle grounds. Startled warriors, animals, and castle retinue began running about crazily as a surprised Morgan and Lathos looked around the compound warily.

"What was *that*?!" Morgan asked, a hint of fear having broken through her sanctimonious façade. "Was bringing the castle down around our ears a part of your grand scheme?"

"Go to the dungeons," Lathos ordered Verthos urgently, "ascertain what has happened! Take some trolls; I want every able-bodied warrior to remain here with me!"

Verthos saluted sharply and ran off to obey his king's command, as faint laughter followed his footfalls. With worried looks on their faces, Morgan and Lathos turned their attention to Thalthas, who was – unlike those around him – apparently pleased with the current situation.

"You wanted to find the Elementals," he said faintly as he eyed Lathos with contempt, his voice growing weaker. "I think *they* have come looking for *you* instead!" Thalthas smiled briefly before slowly lowering his head; and then, he was no more.

*　　*　　*

Angelica kept her hands placed firmly on the wall of the passageway until the last of the tremors subsided. The explosions from the munitions cache had caught all of them off guard, while nearly bringing the roof down on top of them. Instinctively, Angelica had used her abilities to stabilize the earthen walls and rock around them, preventing the entire cavern from caving in.

"Is everyone all right?" she asked as she looked over at her grandmother.

"I...I think so," Tanna answered. She looked around at the prisoners that they had just freed from the cells below for confirmation. They were a bit disoriented and obviously frightened, but otherwise appeared to be unharmed. "Yes, I believe that we are all right!"

"Those explosions," Elwyn exclaimed, "do you think this means..."

"We do not know what it means," Averyil chided him, "so do not jump to any conclusions! Blair is fine – I am sure of it!"

"What of the patrols?" Melas asked anxiously. "They will be upon us soon if we do not move on!"

"I don't think that they will be a problem," Angelica said. "In all of the excitement, I must have forgotten to secure the section of passages that they were in."

Gailon made his way toward the front of the tunnel. He surveyed it for damage before turning to Elwyn. "The corridor appears to be secure; can you lead us out of here? And if so, where will we end up? The castle...the courtyard?"

Elwyn stood there quietly, lost in despair until Averyil's hand lightly touching his arm brought him around. "This passage," he said dully, "will lead us to the courtyard..."

"The courtyard?!" Melas barked. "We will surely be spotted by your brother's men if we try to escape that way! Why can you not use this *portal* of yours to free us?"

"I will not use a portal and leave my sister here alone if there is the slimmest chance that she might be able to join us! If you wish, you could always return to the cells." Elwyn growled.

"Stop it!" Tanna ordered. "This nonsense is getting us nowhere! If the courtyard is our only means of escape, then the courtyard it is! Lead on, Elwyn."

Elwyn nodded his head and, with Angelica by his side, took the lead position. Tanna allowed several of the prisoners to pass her before taking her place in the middle of the formation, while Averyil and Gailon took up the rear.

They moved forward silently; unsure of what might await them around the next turn. Elwyn ambled on as if he were an automaton, going through the motions as though nothing mattered to him any longer. Angelica reached for his hand, concerned about his well-being, and was distressed at how empty his eyes seemed when he looked at her.

"Elwyn," she asked, "are you okay?"

"The truth?" he answered. "No, I am not okay. This – all of this – is my fault. My brother has aligned himself with our enemies, my father is dead; and now I fear that my mother and sister are, as well." The grief she now saw in his eyes brought tears to her own. "All of this woe," he continued, "is because of me. Because of my childish jealousy. Because I did not possess the strength to fight Morgan le Fay and her magic. Now, all of Gorias is lost. Because of me."

"That's not true!" Angelica argued. "Sure, you got yourself into some trouble; and there's a lot that you have to atone for, but *this* isn't your fault! Lathos, Morgan, Shlogg – they're the ones who have caused all of this. As for Blair and Nionia, we just don't know yet. You can't allow yourself to give up hope. You can't afford to!"

"Thank you, Angelica, for your kind words; but I dare say that it is history, and not you, that will be my judge."

Angelica gave his hand a squeeze and was about to reassure him when she heard a noise from within the tunnel. The sound echoed from the darkness in front of them and was evidently heard by Elwyn also, as he raised his hand to signal the group to halt. Tanna came forward, her expression one of confusion, until Angelica pointed to the shadows on the walls of the dimly lit passageway that were advancing toward them.

They breathed a sigh of relief when Erik's large, demonic form turned the corner. He stopped short when he saw them, but a toothy grin cut a slash across his face when recognition kicked in. He came closer, followed by Merlin, Zoe, Annalise, and Eryn. Held tightly within the coils of his tail was the Rider from the woods – Verthos.

"Well," Tanna said as she gave Merlin a hug, "aren't you a sight for sore eyes!" She glanced over at Verthos, who was struggling to free himself. "What's all this?"

"Erik used my memories of this place to provide us with a portal here," Merlin answered as Gailon pushed past him to embrace his granddaughters. "We weren't sure if you needed any help. When we arrived, we found this cowardly sod, along with a group of troll warriors, making their way down here. Suffice it to say, they didn't make it."

"We are headed for the surface," Gailon said as he gave Zoe and Annalise one last squeeze. "Having you all with us should increase our odds of escape! You can provide us with a portal..."

"We *have* to go topside," Zoe told her grandfather, "they have Thalthas!"

"She speaks the truth!" Verthos grunted. "There will be no escape for *any* of you once King Lathos..."

"Do you wish to keep your tongue?" Erik hissed as he hefted the Rider into the air. "If so, I suggest that you remain quiet!" Verthos swallowed audibly and became still.

"The exit is just this way," Merlin said as they made their way through the tunnel once again, "but I must admit that Verthos is correct; we will have a fight on our hands when we reach the courtyard." He glanced around at the assorted faces and then leaned into Tanna.

"Where are Blair and Nionia?" he whispered. "Aren't they with you?"

Tanna did not answer; shaking her head slowly before nodding toward Elwyn. It only took a moment for her meaning to become clear.

"I see...," he said sadly.

"The staff...?" Tanna asked fretfully, hoping to change the subject.

Merlin spat upon the ground. "Morgan has it!" he said bitterly.

They made their way to the surface, exiting out into a courtyard mired in chaos and utter confusion. Soldiers, men on horseback, servants and the like ran about in every direction. Fires had broken out in several different areas due to the cascade of underground explosions, and now, soldiers with buckets of water were attempting to douse the flames.

The prisoners, now free from their cells and once again exposed to the light of the sun, scurried off in any and every direction; losing themselves amongst the bedlam, as people continued to dash about all around the compound. "This may be a good thing," Merlin said as he began waving everyone from the tunnel, "we can use the pandemonium to our advantage!"

"Archers!" someone yelled as they caught sight of Erik; his enormous form easily identifiable through the smoke and tumult that consumed the courtyard. It did not take long for a large number of soldiers – armed with bow and arrow, sword, and spear – to rush into the quadrangle, and surround the hulking demon and the others. Unarmed, Elwyn glared at his brother's troops, as the soldiers readied their weapons.

"Hold your fire!" Lathos commanded loudly as he and Morgan le Fay made their way through the skirmish line. He made a point to stay as close to his warriors as possible; relishing the advantage that he now possessed. "It seems that I have won the day, after all!"

"Not if you have sold your soul!" Elwyn said angrily.

Lathos laughed. "Brother, you have no right to talk to *me* about the selling of one's soul!"

"*I* was placed under a spell," Elwyn argued. "It took magic to make me behave like a fool. What is *your* excuse?"

"My, my...," Morgan purred as she cradled Merlin's magical relic in her arms, "such anger for a prince of Gorias!"

"He is *not* a prince," Lathos growled, "he is a traitor; and we all know what happens tp traitors!" He pointed over his shoulder at the lifeless body of Thalthas; still suspended on the rack.

"You are going to pay for that!" Erik roared.

"You will tell your *pet* to be silent," Lathos said to Elwyn as he purposefully kept his eyes averted from Erik and the others. "You will also instruct it to release my Commander General, at once!"

Erik took Verthos and looked him in the eye before hurling him up, and over, the assembled soldiers. The young Rider screamed as he disappeared momentarily from view before hitting the ground with a loud thud.

"Enough of this," Morgan snarled as she stared at Annalise and the other Elementals hungrily, "give your men the order! Kill them where they stand!"

Lathos nodded in agreement and raised his hand; signaling the archers to prepare their bows. "I wish there were another way, brother..."

The ground began to shake violently once again, causing those within the archers' ranks to stumble and lose their footing. Lathos and Morgan were caught off guard, as well; as the earth split open before them, spewing forth a giant ball of fire that shot straight up into the air.

The massive orb of flame arced mid-air, and then came crashing down. It hit the ground several feet away from Elwyn and the others; the impact sending a concussion wave of heat and debris in every direction. When the dust settled, Elwyn's party had grown by three – as Blair, Nionia, and Alron now stood amongst them.

Alron stepped forward, his dark eyes burning into those of a shocked, and terrified Lathos. He pulled his gaze away from his son, turning instead toward the astonished soldiers who stared at him in disbelief. He was silent only long enough to ensure that he had their undivided attention.

"You *will* stand down," he called out boldly. "I, King Alron, command it!"

12. The Book of E'lythmarium

One by one, all of the soldiers within the courtyard dropped their weapons to the ground and lowered themselves upon bended knee. Their king, once thought dead, was now standing here before them alive and well. One could see that he had been abused; he was bloodied and bruised, but he had returned. Alron, the one true ruler of Gorias, had returned from the dead. Lathos, engulfed in rage, turned and glared at Morgan; the look in his eyes clearly that of a deranged man.

"This is all *your* fault, you spiteful witch!" he exclaimed bitterly. "This is one of your tricks – some foul magic that you have conjured up just to ruin me!"

"The only thing your sorceress is responsible for is having a hand in my imprisonment," Alron barked, "an act in which I feel *you* are equally guilty!"

"N-no, father...," Lathos stammered as he approached Alron, but the king backed away in disgust. "You do not understand! I- I was bewitched...! Yes! Bewitched, like Elwyn – with no control over my actions!"

"You enlisted the aid of dark magic," Alron growled as he ignored his son's pleas, "allied yourself with our enemies; you imprisoned your mother – YOUR MOTHER!"

"Father," Lathos whispered, "please...!"

"You have tortured or killed those who were once loyal to our banner, and in so doing, you have defiled the tribe of Gorias! For the life of me, I cannot think of a punishment that would be suitable enough to fit your crimes."

"My crimes?!" Lathos spat, seeming to find a spine at last. "*My* crimes?! What of *your* crimes, old man? You have been lying within a bed blanketed with your own cowardice the majority of your reign. An entire world awaits us – waiting to be ruled; ruled by the Sidhe! And you, all you ever did was sit upon your throne whining about peace! Well, look around you, father! I have achieved your vaunted peace, and I did it by force. By bringing your dogs to heel. *I* am the true king of Gorias. Long live Lathos!"

Alron and the others stared at the raving young man as he babbled on crazily. Alron shook his head sorrowfully as the stark realization of what Lathos had become took hold. Nearly speechless, he gestured to the men gathered around.

"Seize him," the king said sadly.

"No," Lathos whispered fearfully as he watched the soldiers slowly move in on him. One of the men closest to him reached out for him, but Lathos grabbed his arm and yanked him off balance. The warrior tried to regain his footing, but not before Lathos kneed him in the midsection. As the soldier doubled over, Lathos snatched his sword and tore off toward the castle.

"Lathos!" Elwyn yelled savagely before he ran off in pursuit of his brother.

"After them!" Alron ordered as his men raced toward the castle. "Bring Lathos back to me unharmed!"

The soldiers were mere yards behind Elwyn when an abrupt burst of bright light blinded everyone within the courtyard. When his vision cleared, Alron could see his sons as they disappeared inside the castle. The soldiers, however, were nowhere to be seen.

"I am *so* sorry," Morgan said disapprovingly, "but although it would seem that my partnership with your son has been annulled, I cannot allow your men to take him into custody."

"Where are my warriors?" Alron demanded as he turned on Morgan. "What have you done with them?"

"No need to worry yourself," Morgan said with a flip of her hand. "They are unharmed. I merely returned them to their respective tribal homes. That just leaves you," she said as she pointed the staff in Alron's direction, "and your merry band of misfits for me to deal with."

"Deal with...?" Nionia asked as she joined her husband by his side.

"Of course," Morgan replied as she glared at the queen of Gorias. "You do not think that I plan on leaving any of you alive, do you?"

Before Alron could respond, a second blast of intense light engulfed the courtyard. Morgan lowered her arms, which she had used to shield her eyes from the flash; and as she did, she was mildly surprised to find Alron and the other Sidhe gone. All that remained to face her were Merlin, Erik, and the Elementals.

"Alron and his friends," Morgan said as she eyed the group, "I assume they have been spirited away to someplace safe?"

"They are safe," Erik answered. "You aren't the only one who knows that spell, witch."

"So it would seem," Morgan said as her lip curled in disgust. "I am impressed, demon."

"You should be," Erik growled. "I have a great teacher."

"Yes, about that...," Morgan said as she looked into Merlin's eyes, "...it is about time that we stopped playing this little game. Would you not agree, Merlin?"

"And what game would that be?" Merlin asked.

"Please," Morgan laughed, "you must know by now that I am well aware of your lack of powers! With the staff now in my possession, forcing your – beast – to tell me the location of the Book of E'lythmarium will be pure child's play! So, Merlin...shall we finish this?"

Erik launched himself at the sorceress and was immediately hit with a pulse of electricity from the staff. The surge of spectral energy slammed into his chest and hurled him up and away from Merlin and the others; slamming him to the ground several yards away.

"Your turn!" Morgan hissed as she turned toward Merlin. She pointed the staff at him and sent a second wave of destructive energy in his direction.

Angelica dropped to the ground, slapping the surface with her hand; and in so doing, caused a slab of rock, tall and immensely thick, to shoot up out of the earth in front of the wizard. Morgan's spell crashed into the slab, shattering it into a million pieces. Annalise and Zoe raced to Merlin's aid; and were by his side before the dust could settle while Eryn, Blair, and Angelica moved in on Morgan.

"I'll take care of Merlin," Zoe said to her sister quickly, "you go help the others and get that staff back!"

"Be careful!" Annalise said as she gave Merlin's arm a quick squeeze, and then she ran off to face Morgan with the others.

"Are you all right?" Zoe asked Merlin as she gave him a quick once over.

"I'm fine," he said hurriedly. "Go see to Erik – we're going to need him!"

Zoe rushed over to Erik, who was making his way slowly to his feet. The flesh on his chest was charred and he moved about gingerly, hissing through his teeth with every step that he took. Bewildered, her eyes grew wide with shock; this was the first time that she had ever seen him injured so gravely while in demon form.

"E-Erik...I...are you...?"

"I will pull through," he grunted as he moved past her, "right after I wrap my hands around her throat!"

"No!" Zoe said as she grabbed him by the arm. "Merlin needs you!"

Reluctantly, he pulled his eyes away from the battle going on across the courtyard and looked at Zoe. "Take me to him."

She led him to Merlin, who was supporting himself against a wall of one of the outbuildings. The wizard looked dazed and careworn but steadied himself as he saw them approaching.

"Done playing games?" he huffed as he stared at Erik.

"Merlin," Erik said as he knelt down beside his mentor, "are you all right?"

"Would you all stop asking me that!" he barked. "I need to know boy, can you communicate telepathically with Annalise?"

Erik gave Zoe a confused look before he answered. "I've never tried to reach out to her that way before, but I am sure, if I tried, I could..."

"Excellent," Merlin said. "I have an idea!"

Annalise picked herself up from out of the dirt; wiping away a trickle of blood from the corner of her mouth with the back of her hand. She watched, concerned, as Eryn went flying over her head, landing on the ground with a thud. Staggering to her feet, Eryn took a few clumsy steps before she signaled to Annalise that she was okay. As her friend darted off to return to the fray, Annalise remained behind, nodding her head slowly while she listened to Erik's urgent message as it blared in her head.

She mentally acknowledged Erik before leaping from the ground, flying at Morgan at break-neck speed. Annalise whizzed around the sorceress, swooping this way and that, in an effort to distract and disorient the witch while allowing her friends some time to regroup. The endeavor paid off; Morgan launched attack after attack at the Aether without landing a single blow. Clearly frustrated, Morgan began firing off even more powerful bursts of energy in every direction in the hopes of hitting Annalise; and with each miss, her rage intensified.

"By the Gods, I hate *all* of you!" she spat as she fired another volley at Annalise. "But I despise *you* most of all. I promised myself that I would save you for last – I truly want to see if you will scream as loudly as your mother did when I took her life!"

"What did you say?" Annalise asked as she continued her cat-and-mouse game with the witch. A sickening feeling gripped her as the memory of what Gailon had told her about her parents crept into the far reaches of her mind, but she could not allow herself to become distracted. One wrong move and Morgan would finish her.

"You heard me!" Morgan cackled as she realized that she had struck a nerve. "*I* am the shapeshifter who killed your parents!"

Annalise was in the witch's face in a flash, her hands on the staff as the two struggled to take it from the other. She could feel Morgan's breath against her cheek as they grappled for control of the relic, and the look in Morgan's eyes froze the blood in the girl's veins.

"I warned you," the witch hissed, "you and your friends, that there would be a price to pay for interfering with me! Your father did not know what hit him, but your mother – your mother screamed like a scalded cat!"

Unable to contain her anger, Annalise tightened her grip upon the staff and shot up into the sky. Dark clouds began to coalesce around her and Morgan as they rose higher and higher, and the boom of thunder could be heard from deep within the darkening sky. Annalise's eyes burned with an anger more intense than the heat of the sun as she came to a sudden stop, using her momentum to hurl Morgan back toward the earth beneath them. As the sorceress plunged to the ground, Annalise locked eyes with the other Elementals down below.

"Hit her with everything you've got!"

The staff glowed an eerie shade of green as Morgan utilized its power to slow her descent. She glided gracefully to the ground; her triumphant laughter ringing out over the peals of thunder that crashed up in the sky. She could see the other Elementals as they raced toward her and she stood her ground, eager for the confrontation.

Blair immediately blocked off any path of escape for Morgan by encircling her within a ring of fire. The flames rose up around the witch higher and higher, forming a tower over twenty feet in height. Morgan laughed at the futile attempt and raised her staff up above her head. With a wave of the powerful relic, the flames were snuffed out as quickly as they had appeared. Blair cocked an eyebrow in surprise, but undeterred, conjured up the flames again.

"Can you not see that you are wasting your time?" Morgan crowed as she extinguished the flames a second time. "While I hold the staff I am un...!"

The shifting of the dirt beneath her feet cut her off as four thick, jagged rock walls rose up out of the ground all around her. The slabs of rock rose up toward the sky, and then, one by one fell down atop of the sorceress. As the dust slowly settled, Angelica and Blair walked over to the pile of stone. The flashes of lightning in the darkened sky above them only seemed to enhance the gruesome scene before them.

"I-I've n-never killed a person before...!" Angelica said as her voice quivered with emotion. "I didn't know what else to do. So help me, I didn't know what else to do!"

"You did what you had to," Blair said as she reached out for her friend's hand. "You saw her; saw what she was capable of. She wasn't going to stop. This is for the best, believe me!"

There was a loud crack and then an explosion of rock and debris, as Morgan shot up into the air standing upon a pillar of stone. The pedestal carried her up some fifty feet before coming to a halt; the witch apparently unharmed and glaring down at Angelica and Blair. She took the staff and pointed at the two girls, but before she could cast her spell she was hit with what felt like a hurricane-force wind.

Eryn directed the tempest at Morgan, attempting to knock her from the top of the pillar, but the evil enchantress used the staff to anchor herself in place. The wind howled all around her, whipping her hair into her face, but there was no hiding the demented look in her eyes as she grasped the relic in her hands and lifted it up above her head.

"You Elementals should never have come here," she bellowed over the shrieking of the wind. "Casting your lot with Merlin has only guaranteed your fate! I will, most assuredly, make sure that your deaths are painful ones!"

Morgan began mouthing an ancient curse, determined to put the girls down once and for all. As the forces of time and space began to bend around her, Erik shot up and over the craggy rock face that she stood upon. His massive hands wrapped around her, pinning her arms – and the staff – firmly against her body. The huge demon carried her up into the dark, stormy sky; his wings beating furiously as he carried her higher and higher.

"Annalise!" he yelled over the ear-splitting crash of thunder. "I'm in position. You must strike – NOW!"

Annalise stared down at Erik as the clamor of thunder boomed all around her. She ignored her friend –

focusing only on the evil that was struggling within his grasp. White-hot anger surged within her as she raised her hand above her head. The air crackled with energy as she absorbed the full force of the storm around her. A massive ball of electricity formed above her head; mimicking a small sun as it grew in size and strength. When she felt that the ball lightning had reached its full destructive potential she unleashed it, hurling it headlong at Erik and his captive.

The world seemed to explode around him in a splash of blinding white light. The wave of energy was so extreme that he was far beyond feeling anything akin to pain. Time seemed to stand still, but after a few seconds – or maybe it was an eternity, he was not sure which – he opened his eyes and realized that he was lying on the ground. His vision came back slowly, and as it did he could see Merlin's staff on the ground beside him. Erik reached for the relic and was surprised to see that he was now in his human form. The staff now in his possession, he had no sooner wrapped his fingers around it when a foot came crashing down upon his hand.

"Did you really think that your infantile attempt at stopping me would actually work?" Morgan snarled as she ground her foot painfully on Erik's hand. "You have failed boy! You and your intolerable group of misfits have failed!

Now, you are going to pay the price for that failure. You are going to pay with your life!"

*   *   *

Lathos raced up the stairs to the very top of Castle Thoron's southeast battlement – the castle's tallest tower. He used his shoulder to barrel through the door; and then, tossing his sword to the side, he hauled the lone cannon over and used it to brace the opening shut. The artillery gun was extremely heavy, but in his crazed state, he pushed it into place with ease. He retrieved his weapon and looked over the side of the parapet at the fracas in the courtyard far below. The Elementals were giving Morgan le Fay quite the run for her money; the scene below him resembled that of the Titans facing off against Zeus and the immortals. He was not exactly sure who would prevail, and frankly, at this point, he was beyond caring.

All of his hopes, dreams, and aspirations – all of them were now in ruins because of the witch and her infernal obsession with the Book of E'lythmarium. How he wished that he had been more clear-sighted when she first approached him with her plot to make him king. He had been a fool trusting in her so completely; to throw all of his common sense to the wind and fall under the spell of her web of lies. Now his father was in pursuit – his men biting at Lathos' heels. They would surely capture him, but before they did he wanted to stand here and watch Morgan fall.

The acrid odor of ozone filled his nostrils, and he turned to see his brother as he stepped from the portal. Elwyn stood there, all alone, as the rift closed behind him; the look on his face wounded and angry. Lathos searched within his soul for some emotion – some sense of a bond with his younger brother – but found nothing. He had no more feeling in his heart for Elwyn then he would for a gnat. As he stared at his brother, he wondered *when* he had stopped caring about him; and in the end, he finally decided that it did not matter. Nothing mattered any longer.

"So," Lathos chuckled, "come to take me back to father? It will not place you back within his good graces, you know – he hates you for what you did just as much as he hates me right now!"

"You are wrong," Elwyn argued, "father does not hate us…"

"Oh, for goodness...! Will you wake up!" Lathos spat.

"I know that I have a lot to answer for," Elwyn said as he glared at his brother, "and more than likely I will not be forgiven. If that is to be my lot in this life, then so be it. What I want to know is: Why? Why did you do all of this?"

Lathos stared at his brother with dubious eyes. "You *are* mocking me, surely? Why else would I do *any* of this? For the power! You know what that tastes like – *feels* like – do you not, brother?"

"My lust for power was induced by your witch," Elwyn said. "Gorias would have *been* yours one day..."

"Yes," Lathos said scornfully, "once father had passed on; and who knows when that would have occurred. I simply tried to lend Fate a helping hand."

"The mere fact that you were thinking such a thing is, in and of itself, contemptible!"

"Oh, spare me!" Lathos said, annoyed. "You stand there – with the feelings that you harbored over father and his dreams of peace – and dare to lecture me? You are a joke!"

"I admit," Elwyn said sadly, "that I had my doubts about father and his plans for unification; but I see now that he was right. Even though I had those feelings, I would have *never* had acted upon them on my own. He is my father, and my king!"

"Well," Lathos growled, "he is not mine!" He moved away from the parapet, approaching his brother with an air of haughtiness in his step. Elwyn eyed his sibling's weapon warily, and the fear in his eyes made Lathos smile. "Father has been, and always will be a fool! The Elementals fall into his lap – the single greatest weapon in all of the universe – and he welcomes them with a party! Seriously?! I would have enslaved them immediately and then used them to lay waste to my enemies!"

"One of those of whom you would have enslaved is your sister," Elwyn pointed out as he began to slowly back away from his brother.

"What of it?" Lathos barked. "Yara was born to serve a purpose. She is a weapon – nothing more. *I* would have put her, *and* her abilities, to use properly!"

"I hear your words, brother; but I can not believe that you would treat family that way!"

"Believe it!" Lathos laughed.

"And mother...?" Elwyn asked, standing fast and no longer retreating. "What of her?"

"M-mother...?" Lathos stammered, his voice faltering as he slowly lowered his weapon. "W-what do you mean?"

"You have expressed your feelings for me, father, and Yara," Elwyn said slowly as he studied his brother, "but you have not mentioned our mother – not once. I can only assume that..."

"I would *never* have hurt mother!" Lathos said indignantly. "For you to even suggest such a thing shows just how little you truly know me!"

Elwyn approached his brother slowly, his hands open in an act of appeasement. He believed that he saw an opening, a chink in his brother's armor, and he wished to exploit it. "My apologies, truly! It is just that you had her imprisoned – *that* is somewhat hard to explain. Do you not agree?"

"Not at all," Lathos stated defensively. "I had her held for her own protection!"

"Her...protection?"

"Of course," Lathos explained. "Morgan and Shlogg were adamant – anything or anyone, which lent credence to Alron and his rule was to be destroyed. It was not long before their spiteful eyes turned toward mother. I knew that her days were numbered, so hoping to spare her life, I had her placed in the dungeons. The act seemed to pacify them, and mother was safe."

"So," Elwyn said as he continued moving cautiously toward Lathos, "there is a place for *mother* in a world ruled by you?"

"Of course there is," Lathos said. His voice sounded heavy, as though he had become incredibly exhausted. His shoulders drooped, and he returned to the parapet; his younger brother forgotten as he placed a shaky hand upon the stone ledge for support. "Or should I say 'was.' Mother means the world to me. My rule would have been meaningless without her love and support."

Elwyn eyed his brother suspiciously; unsure of what to think or to say.

"Did you know that she was aware of your having nightmares?" Lathos asked as he glanced at Elwyn. His eyes looked tired, as though the light had gone out of them.

"You told her about them?"

"I did not have to – that is mother. She has a way of knowing these things."

"Yes," Elwyn agreed as he made his way to the parapet, as well. Lathos' anger seemed to have melted away, but Elwyn still kept his eye on his brother's weapon. "I could never hide anything from her."

"Nor could I," Lathos said. He looked out at the courtyard once more as the skies grew dark and thunder boomed in the distance. When next he spoke, his voice was little more than a whisper. "I have been a fool..."

Elwyn watched his brother, saying nothing. It was as if all of the fight had gone out of him. This Lathos – the quiet, thoughtful man standing beside Elwyn now – was the closest thing to the brother that he remembered for quite some time.

Lathos continued, his words quiet and remorseful. "I have destroyed everything, Elwyn. I have destroyed Gorias, our tribe's reputation amongst the other Sidhe – and just about everything that mother and father have held dear."

"It is not as terrible as it seems, brother," Elwyn said as he finally let down his guard; placing an encouraging hand upon Lathos' shoulder. "What has been destroyed can always be rebuilt again."

"Yes," Lathos said as he turned to face Elwyn, "but why would I want to do that?"

Without warning, Lathos grabbed Elwyn's arm and pulled his younger brother toward him, plunging his sword into him. Eyes wide with shock, Elwyn gasped as the blade was pushed through his body; his eyes locked with Lathos'. Surprise turned into white-hot pain as the blade ripped through muscle and tissue; finally bursting through the back of Elwyn's armor wet with blood.

"Tell me, brother; what truly hurts more?" Lathos asked darkly as he leaned into his brother's side to whisper into his ear. "My blade buried within your gut or the fact that you foolishly placed your trust in me once again? You are so incredibly gullible! All I needed to do was whimper and moan about our poor, dear mother and you pranced right up to me like a lamb to the slaughter!"

"You...you did not...have to do this," Elwyn winced.

"Oh, but I did," Lathos said as Elwyn's blood poured out onto his hand. "And I will do the same to Father and Yara, as well; but do you want to know what I *truly* regret?"

Elwyn tried to focus on his brother's voice, a voice that sounded like it was coming from the far side of a long, dark tunnel. He coughed, and blood sprayed across Lathos' face; embellishing his already ghastly appearance.

"What I will truly regret," Lathos whispered, "is that you will not be here to watch me slay Nionia!"

Elwyn stared at his brother as the life flowed from his body. He brought his arms up, as a tear rolled down his cheek, and wrapped them around Lathos in a final embrace.

"There there, brother." Lathos sighed quietly as Elwyn held him close. "It is time for you to sleep. There is no reason to fear the darkness; for now, it will be your friend for all eternity!"

"I will not...fear the darkness," Elwyn said slowly as his grip tightened around Lathos' waist, "because I will not be alone!"

Before Lathos could stop him, Elwyn lifted his brother from the ground; pushing him forward and up against the wall of the parapet. Off balance, Lathos began to flail his arms, which only propelled both of them over the side of the tower. Lathos cried out as he felt himself falling through space; his arms and legs thrashing about wildly.

Elwyn pulled his brother closer, holding onto him with the last bit of strength remaining within him. He knew that the ground was fast approaching – soon he would have the rest that Lathos had promised, but he would not let it end like this. He would not leave their broken bodies to be found by their parents. They did not deserve that.

With his dying breath, Elwyn uttered the words that opened a portal beneath them. The pungent odor alerted Lathos to his brother's actions, and his eyes bulged in terror as he realized Elwyn's intent.

"No, Elwyn!" Lathos shrieked. "Not this way! Not this way!"

Elwyn breathed his last as they entered the inky rift; his vacant eyes eternally locked upon Lathos' face. Lathos' screams became lost within the folds of time and space as the portal closed behind them with a pop – and with that, the sons of Alron were no more.

*   *   *

Morgan reached down and snatched the staff from Erik's hand. She inspected the relic briefly to ensure that it was undamaged, and then stared down at Erik. He returned her gaze calmly; his face emotionless as he looked up at her lazily. Thrown off by his seemingly uncaring attitude, she eyed him curiously before removing her foot from his hand. She looked around for the Elementals, but oddly enough they were nowhere to be seen.

"Of the lot of you," Morgan said hesitantly, "I always thought you the most peculiar of the bunch. Here you are, moments from death, and you lie there with that empty-headed look on your face!"

"Oh," Erik said casually, "I'm not about to die..."

"You think not?" Morgan sneered. "And why is that?"

"You're gonna be way too busy dealing with him," Erik said as he pointed to something behind her.

Morgan grinned at Erik – not one to fall for the old deception – when a thick, leathery tail wrapped itself around her waist. She barely had enough time to acknowledge her plight before she was snatched up and dragged across the ground. Morgan grabbed at the tail, dropping the staff in the process, as she struggled to free herself.

Erik scrambled up and ran over to retrieve the magical relic as the demon that once resided within him collected its prize. The creature lifted Morgan up into the air and glared at her for a moment, confused. It did not stay that way for long, however; as it quickly realized that she had been the one who had burned its chest with her magic. The beast roared mightily as it spread its wings; the anger in its eyes more than apparent.

Erik ran over to where Merlin and the girls were hiding; the staff theirs once again. He handed the relic over to Merlin, gasping wildly; his bravado from just moments ago completely spent. He stared at his mentor wildly as the wizard reclaimed his staff.

"Did the lightning strike *have* to be so massive?" he cried. "I *hate* being struck by lightning!"

"Pish posh," Merlin said as he savored the weight of the relic in his hands once again. "The lightning was necessary in order to split the demon and you apart. You should be pleased that my plan worked out so well."

"You told me to recite the incantation," Erik said angrily, "and that Morgan would be the one that was to be hit!"

"Are you really going to stand there and quibble over such a minor detail?" Merlin said absently.

"We don't have time for this," Annalise said as she watched the confrontation going on in front of them. Morgan had freed herself from the demon's grasp and was casting spell after spell at the monster. "They're nearly on top of us!"

"Right you are," Merlin agreed. He placed a hand on Erik's shoulder and looked him in the eye. "Are you ready, lad? What we're about to do will make that lightning strike feel like a feather's caress."

"I don't really have a choice — do I?" Erik asked nervously.

"Not this time I'm afraid," Merlin said soberly.

"Will Erik be okay, Merlin?" Zoe asked, worried.

"Oh, Master Hedley won't feel a thing," Merlin said.

"But you said that...," Zoe began.

"Erik won't feel a thing," Merlin repeated. "*I*, on the other hand, am about to absorb the arcane abilities of the most powerful witches and warlocks known to wizard-kind. I dare say that it will be comparable to walking into a solar flare – and *that's* putting it mildly."

"But Erik was in no danger when you hid the Book of E'lythmarium inside his head," Angelica said. "Why would you be?"

"Erik was possessed by a demon," Merlin said looking at her. "He was protected by the creature's dark magic. I no longer have my magic. There is nothing to protect me if this goes wrong."

"But I'm no longer possessed," Erik said.

"One more reason," Merlin said gravely, "why we must remove the Book from within you as quickly as possible." He looked at each of them as though he was never going to see them again. "You all have done so much, more than I ever had the right to ask of you. I put you all at risk more times than I can count – that ends here. This fight is mine now. I started all of this – it's time that I finished it!" Merlin hefted the staff and squared his shoulders back. "Do you know the incantation?" he asked Erik.

"Yes," Erik answered. "I know the one!"

"Then let us begin. Ladies," Merlin said softly, "step back if you please."

Morgan dodged another blow from the demon's tail, and in so doing, tripped and fell to the ground. She rolled over onto her back, casting a quick spell that sent hundreds of shards of rock flying at the creature. The hulking monster cried out in pain as the sharp pieces of stone pierced its skin and eyes. Temporarily blinded, the monster began stomping upon the ground in an attempt at crushing the sorceress under its feet.

Morgan jumped out of the brute's path and searched for a place to hide while the demon was without its sight, but her reprieve was short-lived. The demon pulled its fists away from its bloodied face and scanned the courtyard in search of the witch. It quickly located her, making its way toward her as it growled angrily. The creature's lips were pulled back in a vicious snarl; revealing a row of huge, deadly fangs.

The sorceress was about to unleash one final spell – one that would either finish off the beast or leave her at its mercy – when the entire world went blindingly white once again. Both she and the demon shielded their eyes from the blast of light; the monster roaring in pain due to the garish flash. Darkness quickly followed the explosive brilliance of light, and an immense wind nearly knocked both combatants off their feet.

"What magic is this?!" Morgan screamed through the howling of the wind. She had barely withstood the onslaught that Eryn had unleashed upon her – this was ten times that. The demon, too, roared in protest at the sudden storm that had fallen upon them seemingly from nowhere.

"What magic is this?" a voice answered loudly, echoing all around them and throughout the courtyard. "What magic *is* this? Why, Morgan – it is the magic that you have craved all of your life!"

"No!" Morgan shuddered fearfully. "Not the magic of E'lythmarium!" She searched the darkness, but the only thing that she could see was the demon as it battled and clawed at the wind in vain before it leaped into the air to escape the fury of the storm. "The magic of E'lythmarium was to be mine!" Morgan shouted madly. "Mine; do you hear?!"

The wind continued to howl all around her – taunting her as it whipped her first in one direction and then another. "That is my book!" Morgan railed. "I demand that you return it to me at once! The book is mine! The book is *mine!*"

"Do you truly want the book?" the booming voice echoed. "Are you sure? If you want it so badly, then by all means – come and take it!"

Merlin floated through the darkness toward Morgan; the Book of E'lythmarium in his hands. Morgan made her way through the gusting winds, scrambling through the maelstrom toward her prize. For every step that she took the wind would push her back two, and Merlin began to laugh at her and her hopeless folly.

"Do not laugh at me!" she ranted crazily. "I am Morgan le Fay! You *will* fear me! Once the Book is mine you will bow before me! Give me back my book!"

"The book," Merlin hissed menacingly, "is indeed yours! Here – come claim your prize!"

The wizard opened the book, holding its pages out for Morgan to see. Fear gripped her as she read the words, discernment bringing about a sudden clarity as the words written on the pages leaped out at her; and in a panic, she turned to flee. The wind that had been pushing her *away* from the book abruptly changed direction – now pulling her toward it instead. Morgan fell to the ground, shrieking in terror as she clawed at the dirt. The wind continued to pull her, kicking and screaming, toward the Book of E'lythmarium.

"Come, Morgan," Merlin said loudly, "come and see what the Book of E'lythmarium holds for you!"

Morgan felt her body being lifted from the ground, and she screamed as she went hurtling through the air toward Merlin. A strange sound came from within the pages of the book in the wizard's hands; voices crying out as though they were experiencing the worst pain imaginable. The noise grew in volume until it drowned out the howling of the wind; and Morgan, sucked forcefully into the Book of E'lythmarium, quickly joined the voices and their horrible chorus.

As the storm abated, it gave way to mild blue skies; and the brutal winds dwindled to a light breeze. Merlin listened for a moment longer to the wailing and screeching from the tormented souls that came from within the ancient tome, and then he closed the Book of E'lythmarium one last time – its pages never to be opened again.

Epilogue

The room was still as Merlin and Tanna slowly ascended the staircase to the balcony above. The wizard walked over to the balustrade, taking a moment to look down at the faces of his friends who were assembled down below. He could tell by their expressions that they had no idea as to why he and Tanna had summoned them; it was now time to satisfy their curiosity as well as reward their patience.

"Long ago," Merlin began, "I came across a prophecy that foretold the events of the past few months. Some of you know of it, while others have only heard me recite bits and pieces. I now remind you of those ancient words." He paused for a moment, and then said:

"When two eagles rise; one false and one true,

and with Lugh's spear lifted,

nature's warriors will join the fray,

with a demon of magic gifted.

The battle waged on mystic Isle,

and a kinship's truth a lie,

for good to finally win the lance,

a warrior true must die."

He watched them for a second – the room still silent, save for Nionia's sharp intake of breath – before he continued. "We did indeed wage battle, and in the end, good triumphed. But our victory came at a price. Most of us here lost friends. King Alron and Queen Nionia – they lost their sons. Blair – she lost two brothers.

"It is a bittersweet time; one where we celebrate victory over an evil which wished to rule all of Avalon, while we mourn the loss of those whom we loved. And so," Merlin went on as he raised his staff above his head, "it is with this in mind that I wish to leave an enduring reminder for all of Gorias and for those who will visit Castle Thoron in the future."

The tip of the staff glowed warmly as Merlin whispered something under his breath. He then lowered the staff and directed everyone's attention to the space behind them. There were collective gasps and sounds of wonder as his audience moved away from their places below the balcony.

Tanna and Merlin remained on the landing as they watched the scene below. The Elementals, along with Erik, Gailon, Averyil, Alron, and Nionia now gathered around the foot of the golden tree that grew within the entrance of Castle Thoron. They were all looking up reverently as two large eagles, both made of solid gold, circled the tree in an eternal game of follow the leader. They began at the bottom of the tree's lower branches, swirling round and round until they reached the very top of the tree; where they would then make their way back to the bottom to begin the journey all over again. Alron watched the birds stoically as he extended a hand each to Nionia and Blair.

"What a beautiful way to help them remember their sons," Tanna said softly as she wiped a tear from her eye. "If one didn't know any better, they would be forced to assume that you do indeed have a heart."

"Hush now," Merlin smiled as he watched the birds that he had conjured up flying circles around the tree, "you'll give away my secret."

"Do you know what happened to them – Elwyn and Lathos?" Tanna asked. "Is it true that they are lost?"

"If Elwyn did not have a destination in mind when he opened his portal," Merlin answered sadly, "then they are doomed to remain within the shadows of time and space forever."

Tanna shuddered at the thought. She had bore witness to too much pain and sadness these past few weeks. One of the girls was saying something to the royal family; from this distance, Tanna could not make out what was being said, but she was grateful for the distraction that had pulled her thoughts away from Elwyn and Lathos.

"I must speak with King Alron," Merlin said. "Would you care to join me?"

Tanna nodded her head, and they made their way down from the balcony. They descended the staircase and walked over to the great tree. Alron and the others were completely engrossed by the golden birds, so it took a tap upon his shoulder before he realized that she and Merlin were standing there.

"If we might have a moment of your time, your majesty?" Merlin inquired.

"Yes," Alron said thickly, his voice filled with emotion. "Yes, of course." The king excused himself, Nionia mouthing a heartfelt thank you to the wizard as she released her husband's hand, and he followed Merlin and Tanna to the other side of the room.

"Thank you, Merlin. It is a beautiful memorial," Alron said as he shook the wizard's hand.

"It was the least that I could do," Merlin said. "I cannot imagine what you and Nionia must be going through..."

"Yes, we...," Alron swallowed hard before continuing. "...we have our moments."

Merlin nodded his head knowingly. Tanna stepped forward and gave the king a hug.

"It probably is not proper etiquette, but..."

"I am the King," Alron said with a smile, "and I will decide what is proper etiquette!" He returned her warm embrace. "Thank you."

"I wish there was something I could do for Thalthas, as well. Did he have any family?" Merlin asked.

"None, I am afraid. We," Alron said sadly, "were his family."

"He was a true warrior," Tanna acknowledged, "and a good friend."

"Indeed," Alron agreed. "He will be sorely missed."

"Your majesty," Merlin asked now that they had paid their respects, "have you any idea how these events have affected your peace initiatives? Have you received any word from the other tribes?"

"My efforts to make the Sidhe a unified people," Alron said with a measure of disappointment, "have come to naught. I am barely on speaking terms with King Locien, the Murias have not answered any of my correspondence, and the elders of the tribe Falias have not entirely discarded the idea of bringing me up on charges with the High Council."

"Charges?!" Tanna said. "What sort of charges?"

They hold me somewhat responsible for the death of King Korren. They believe that I should have seen Lathos' descent into madness, and done something about it."

"Those charges would not withstand scrutiny with the High Council," Merlin argued.

"I know this," Alron agreed. "They are angry. Their anger will pass with time."

"So we are back where we started," Tanna lamented, "there is to be no real peace between the tribes?"

"I will never give up on my dream," Alron said. "I truly believe that the Sidhe will be one people in the not too distant future." He looked over at Nionia and Blair, who were locked in an embrace. "Now, if you will excuse me..."

Merlin bowed as Alron returned to his family. "Thank you for your time, your majesty."

"That poor man," Tanna said as she watched Alron walk away.

"Yes," Merlin agreed. "It would seem that while the Elementals have dealt with their struggles, they are just beginning for Alron."

"So, as I understand it, the girls are no longer in any danger?"

"The prophecy," Merlin said, "has been fulfilled. It is now safe for the Elementals to return home to Avalon – if they so choose."

"I have spoken to them," Tanna said, "and they have made their decision."

"Go on," Merlin said as he turned to her.

"Angelica and I are staying in Traverse City," Tanna replied, "at least until she graduates. After that, she would like to come to Avalon for a while.

"Annalise and Zoe also wish to remain in Traverse City – at least for now. They're not sure if Avalon holds anything for them. They have family here, of course, and they want to spend time with them; but they have family in Michigan, as well. They are torn and will need some time."

"Of course," Merlin said with a nod of his head. "I completely understand. Perhaps, as they grow older, they will come to call both places home."

"Perhaps," Tanna said. "Eryn has decided that her home is with her mother in Traverse City. I think she said 'Nice place to visit, but I don't want to live here.'"

"I assumed as much," Merlin said. He was silent for a moment before speaking again. "And what of Blair?"

"She is coming with us," Tanna said.

"Is that wise?" Merlin asked. "Surely she realizes that she is the sole heir to the throne of Gorias. She will be Queen one day."

"Yes," Tanna acknowledged, "but not today. She has talked with her parents and they understand completely. She will be visiting them often, and they have invited her to bring her adoptive family to the castle as often as she likes."

"Speaking of which," Merlin said, "it is time that they should be heading back home – since that is what they have decided to do." He smiled warmly at Tanna. "I am glad that you are going back with them. I feel much better knowing that *you* will be there to keep an eye on them. Officers Sims and Eagler are good men, but I can't expect them to babysit six magical beings for the next several years, now can I?"

"Six?" Tanna said curiously. "I do not understand. I thought that the demon and Erik had been separated. Now that he is no longer possessed, how can he be included with the others?"

"A permanent side-effect," Merlin said, "of his having the Book of E'lythmarium locked away in his subconscious all of this time – he now possesses *true* magical ability. I'm afraid to say it, but the lad could one day become even more powerful than me."

"Is he aware of this?" Tanna asked, shocked.

"We've talked. I've made it quite clear that I will be making regular visits to ensure that he becomes a proper wizard."

"I'm sure that he was happy to hear that," Tanna teased.

"Quite," Merlin said as they both laughed.

"So," Tanna went on, "I suppose that this is the end."

"The end...?"

"Yes," she answered, "for Erik and the girls, this is the end of their adventure. They can close this particular book, place it on the shelf, and get on with their lives."

"Oh," Merlin said, "I wouldn't say that their story is over. The tale is simply put on hold until another plot line comes along."

"Merlin," Tanna said suspiciously, "I've seen that look in your eye before! Do you have something up your sleeve?"

"Me?" Merlin said, pretending to be shocked. "Why madam, I'm as innocent as a new born babe. However; if a situation were to arise – say, due to someone accidently freeing a giant dragon hellbent on world domination from its prison...!"

The End

58357096R00181

Made in the USA
Lexington, KY
09 December 2016